The Rulebreaker

real love stories never end

NEW YORK TIMES BESTSELLING AUTHOR
CLAIRE CONTRERAS

Claire Contreras
© 2021 Claire Contreras
Cover design By Hang Le
Edited by Erica Russikoff
Proofread by Janice Owen
Formatted by Champagne Book Design

ISBN: 978-0-9986629-8-5

Without limiting the rights under copyright reserved above, no part of this publication may be reproduced, stored in or introduced into a retrieval system, or transmitted, in any form, or by any means (electronic, mechanical, photocopying, recording, or otherwise) without the prior written permission of the above author of this book.

This is a work of fiction. Names, characters, places, brands, media, and incidents are either the product of the author's imagination or have been used fictitiously. Any resemblance to actual persons, living or dead, events, or locales is entirely coincidental.

The author acknowledges the trademarked status and trademark owners of various products referenced in this work of fiction, which have been used without permission. The publication/use of these trademarks is not authorized, associated with, or sponsored by the trademark owners.

The Rulebreaker

Prologue

Past

Maverick

THE FACT THAT OUR HOCKEY COACH IS MAKING US SIT DOWN and pen letters like we're in the 1930s is the first ridiculous thing about this assignment. The second is that I've been paired up with a girl. A girl who plays soccer, not even hockey. What the hell am I supposed to write? *I hope you don't touch the ball with your hands by mistake?* I sigh heavily and set my pen down for the third time.

"Cruz, you better pick up that pen and start writing like Alexander Hamilton, before I kick you out, or worse, make all of you run an extra mile on your behalf."

There's a collective groan around the room. "Hell no, Coach. Cruz, just write something, anything."

"What the hell am I supposed to write?" I look around at my teammates. "What are you writing, Rogers?"

"That I hope she scores a triple." Rogers shrugs both shoulders.

"You got a softball player?" I frown. "Why did I get a soccer player? I don't know anything about soccer."

"Who cares? The point of this is to learn, to lend an ear to someone who may need it. it's not to recruit each other into your sport," Coach says. "Just ask her how her week was, if she has a dog, I don't care."

"Fine." I sigh again and pick up the pen and start writing.

Her name is Rocky. That's a pretty cool name for a girl, so I start my letter with that.

Prologue Two

Rocky

"That boy I keep writing letters to—"

"The one I don't like?" Dad asks, frowning.

"You don't like any boys, Dad." I roll my eyes. "But yeah, that one."

"What about him?" Mom asks.

"He's going to a sports summer camp this summer."

"A sleep away camp?" Dad's tone already tells me everything I need to know without even asking.

"Mike, let her talk. Jesus." Mom shakes her head, sighing. "What about this camp?"

"It seems pretty cool. They have hockey, soccer,

basketball. It's only like an hour from here, so it's not even that far." I bite my lip. Dad's frown deepens. Mom's face is serious, but I feel like maybe she'd budge. "It's not cheap, but they have scholarships for those of us who can't pay the full price."

"Do you have a brochure?" Mom asks.

"Beverly." Dad starts, but shuts up the moment mom shoots him a look.

"We'll be working all summer, Mike. This may be a good option for all of us."

"And this boy is going?"

"Yeah, but it's not like that, Dad. We're just friends."

"Until he sees you."

"Mike," Mom says.

"It's true. That boy will take one look at her and say he wants more than just friendship. I know how this works."

"Of course, you do." I roll my eyes. "I think I can make my own choices."

"She's right, Mike." Mom shoots him a look. "Do you have his phone number? I want to speak to his parents."

"Ummm . . ." I bite my lip. "Yeah, I think I can get his number."

I've been secretly speaking to Maverick for the last six months. We really are just friends though, which is nice, and contrary to what dad thinks, he's not going to freak out and change his mind when he sees me. We've already also seen each other at the park and spoken there. He's even joined me in soccer matches, so there's absolutely nothing for them to worry about. All my friends have the biggest crush on him, and I get it. Maverick is very cute, but his friendship means so much to me and I wouldn't do anything to jeopardize it, so he'll remain in the friendzone forever as far as I'm concerned.

Chapter One

Rocky

Present

I close my eyes as I sit down on the bench and let out a heavy exhale. I'm so tired. I've been up since five in the morning, which is the norm, but last night I made the grave mistake of going out with some friends and we got home entirely too late for this shit.

"Rocky, are you done with the weight room, or have you not even started?"

"I'm done." I don't even bother to open my eyes. "I'm going home to take a nap."

"Maybe I'll go with you so I can get a glimpse of those hot-ass roommates of yours," Ashley says from across the room.

I laugh, my eyes popping open. "You wouldn't think they're so hot if you actually hung out with them for a day. The only thing they talk about is COD and hockey."

"The only thing we talk about is soccer and hot guys," Ashley says.

"And hot girls," Leyla adds.

"And hot girls," I repeat with a laugh. "I guess we're not so different after all."

"Are they dating anyone?" Leyla asks. "Maverick and Colson, I mean."

"Yeah right." I scoff. "They're forever playing the field."

"I guess they might as well enjoy it while they can," Ash says. "You know, before their penises shrivel up and they can no longer get them up."

"I am so glad I don't have a penis," Leyla says.

"And that you don't like them either," I add.

"True." She laughs.

I grab my bag and swing it onto my shoulder as I stand up, saying bye to my teammates as I walk out of the room and head to my car. According to the time, I have about twenty minutes to myself in the house if I get there as soon as possible. My roommates should be at hockey practice, or at least, their first leg of it. Our schedules coincide in that way. We normally have two practices a day between classes, and because two of us are taking the same online class, it means Maverick and I have the exact same schedule. Colson's is similar, but he helps out at his uncle's pizza shop on the down-low since we're technically not allowed to have paying jobs while we're in school. It's dumb and part of the reason half of the athletes in our university are currently facing jail time, but that's a story for another day. When I pull up to the house, I see Maverick's car parked out front. I lock mine and walk toward the house quickly. I've known Mav since we were ten years old and I've never known him to miss a practice.

"Mav?" I call out as I open the door and shut it behind me.

"In here," he says from the kitchen. His voice sounds congested as hell.

"Oh no." I let my bag fall to the floor by the stairs and finish walking over to the kitchen, where he's sitting in front of a bowl of soup. "You're sick?"

"Yeah." He sniffles. "Fucking sucks."

"So you didn't go to practice?"

"Coach wants me to self-quarantine, you know, because of all the bullshit."

"The bullshit meaning the pandemic?" I back up a step. "Should I be near you?"

"I don't have the virus." He shoots me a dirty look. "I have a cold."

"How do you know?"

"Because I have my vaccines." His brows pull into a frown. "We all do, so there's no need to worry."

He looks so cute when he does that. Not that I'd ever say that to him. My best friend is hot though, what can I say? We made a pact somewhere along the way to never cross that line.

A pact that I am absolutely glad we made because knowing us and our short attention spans, we would have one-thousand percent already broken up and made things awkward.

"Well, let me know if you need anything. I'm going to shower and take a nap before class. I'm so tired."

"You shouldn't have gone out last night." He brings the bowl up and begins slurping the soup.

"I hate that sound." I groan and start walking out of the kitchen.

"You hate every sound. I don't know how you're ever going to find a boyfriend and actually stay with him." Mav sets the bowl down with a chuckle.

"I do not hate every sound and when I find a guy who holds my attention and my love, I will cherish every noise he makes."

Maverick's deep chuckle follows me all the way upstairs. I ignore the way it makes my heart bounce inside my chest, as if it's the most melodic thing I've ever heard. I may suffer from acute misophonia, but that's one sound I'll never grow tired of. As I push my door open and glance at myself in the mirror, I realize I'm smiling. I shake my head with a sigh. I don't think I have actual feelings for Maverick. First of all, this thing where I notice how hot he is, is a recent development. I never felt that way before. I don't know if it happened after we moved in together or maybe I always found him attractive before and just never let myself truly look at him that way. Either way, I don't like it. Maybe if it were Colson I had a physical crush on it would be fine. I haven't known him nearly as long as I've known Mav, and Colson is hot, with his bad boy persona and tattoos, but when I look at him my heart doesn't flutter. I push it out of my mind as I shower and dress in comfortable clothes—soft cotton shorts and one of Maverick's old hockey shirts that fits me like I'm playing dress up with my dad's clothes. The moment I see my unmade bed, I dive in, shut my eyes, and go to sleep.

I'm not sure at which point Maverick comes into my room, but I don't even bother to open my eyes when I feel the bed dip as he gets into my bed. He does this sometimes, just sneaks in here and sleeps beside me. It's something my friends don't think is normal and caused them to speculate that we were hooking up, but honestly, it's not wild at all. We've been doing this since we were teenagers and went to sports camp together and have never even kissed. Even though my feelings are all out of whack, Mav doesn't see me in that way at all and it's better that way.

At least, that's what I'm telling myself.

Chapter Two

"**H**ey, Mom." I beam at the phone screen as my mother's face becomes visible.

"Hey, baby. How was practice this morning?"

"Good. Tiring."

"She stayed out way too late last night," Maverick calls out from somewhere behind me.

"Shut up." I shoot him a glare over my shoulder, but it only makes him chuckle.

"Hi, Ms. Bev," he says quickly.

"Hey, Maverick," she says with a smile even though she can't see him from where I'm sitting around the kitchen counter. "Why were you out late, Rocky? Where'd you go?"

"I wasn't out that late, first of all," I say. "And I went to a party with Leyla."

"Hm. How's she doing?"

"Good. Same as always. Girl crazy."

"I know that's right." Mom laughs. "Did you already have your online class?"

"Yep. Just finished it. I have to go to practice in an hour and then I'm going to work."

"How are those girls treating you? Do they still talk back to you like you're part of their squad and not their elder?"

"Nah, they're nice to me now. I befriended Jos, and the rest of them kind of fell into place. I think they have a crush on Coach Dereck and therefore see me as a threat." I roll my eyes.

"Is Coach Dereck cute?"

"He's very freaking cute actually." I laugh.

Mom laughs. "Well, maybe there's something there."

"Eh." I shrug. "I feel like he would've asked me out by now if he felt that way about me."

"How could anyone not feel that way about you, Rock? You're the most gorgeous girl in the world."

"You say that because I look just like you." I smile. Mom winks.

I do look just like her. My skin is a shade lighter, but my pear-shaped face, plump lips, and high cheekbones are all her. She has dark, tight, ringlet curls that frame her face, and my hair is curly, but definitely not as curly as hers. I get that from Dad, as well as my light green eyes and the annoying freckles that dot my nose and cheeks. I hear movement behind me and see Maverick walking up to me in the camera I'm holding up. He looks so good, his glowing caramel skin making mine look lackluster. He has a pile of brown curls on his hair that he never bothers to do anything about, and when he grins at the phone in my hand, that sexy-and-I-know-it smile of his, I think I may just fall out of the chair. But I don't and I definitely do not let him know I'm affected by any of this.

"When are you going to send us some food, Ms. Bev?" he asks, setting an elbow on the counter beside me and his chin on my shoulder.

"When is your momma going to stop sending you Uber Eats?" Mom raises an eyebrow. "Don't think I don't know about that."

"Aw, does my mom go around telling everyone my business?" He shakes his head, standing upright. I laugh.

"Your business? That's her money," Mom says. "You better start working."

"You know they don't let us." He taps his shoulder against mine.

"Well, you're most likely going pro after this season." I shoot him a pointed look. "Some of us want to get ahead of the game and have something good on our resumes for when the time comes."

"That's my girl," Mom says. "Well, I have to let you go. Your father's due home in thirty minutes and I want to make sure he's fed before he goes back to the hospital for his shift."

"Oh boo, I thought you guys were working the same schedule now?"

"No, honey, there's been some drama in the hospital, so I had to take mornings and he's working evenings. Don't you worry about us. We're both off on Sundays and will still make it to our Sunday ritual." She winks. "Love you, baby."

"Love you too, Ms. Bev," Maverick says before I can answer. We both laugh. I bump his shoulder hard with mine.

"Love you, Mom!"

When we hang up, I sigh heavily.

"You miss her, huh?" Mav asks.

"Yeah." I pout. "I miss having our Sunday rituals in person."

"You'll see her in a couple of weeks." Mav puts an arm around me and gives me a side hug. "But if you need me to go to the movies with you, you know I will."

"Yeah, right. You're the worst." I push him off with a laugh.

"I do not talk that much, Rocky." He tilts his head.

"You talk before, during, and after."

The door opens and closes and Colson comes into view as we're talking.

"What's going on?" He frowns.

"Who is the worst person to watch a movie with?" I ask.

"Maverick. Hands down." Colson laughs, walking toward the fridge. "He doesn't shut the fuck up."

"Thank you," I say proudly.

"Fuck you both," Maverick says with a chuckle. "I'll try to work on that."

"I mean, imagine you end up with a girl who enjoys the movies," I say. "That would be the deal-breaker for her."

"Oh, that would be the deal-breaker?" Maverick asks. "Since you're so knowledgeable on the matter, why don't you school me on things women like?"

"Like that's going to help you get a girl," Colson says, still looking in the fridge. I swear he does this every day, as if something is just going to pop out of there fully cooked for him.

"I get plenty of girls." Mav frowns.

"Yeah, groupies." I snort.

He does, too. We had to make a rule so they'd stop bringing random girls over multiple nights a week. They're now limited to Friday and Saturdays only, and still, it's uncomfortable and awkward for me the morning after since I'm usually in the kitchen making breakfast and have to witness the walk of shame while the guys don't even bother to close the door behind them.

"So help me get a serious one."

"You're serious?" I blink at him.

"One hundred percent."

"Okay," I say slowly.

We shake on it before I realize what time it is and start rushing to the door. As I'm driving back to campus, I start thinking about the deal I just made and wonder what the hell is wrong with me. I don't know the first thing about what women want because I don't even know what I want, but I decide I'll start there. It'll be a lesson for us both.

Chapter Three

"**C**OACH, CAN YOU CALL TIME?" PEYTON ASKS.

I look at my watch. "Twenty seconds."

There's a collective groan. While we're waiting for Coach Dereck, who's running late, I have the girls doing their normal drills, including wall squats. The worst, I know, but they're necessary to build the endurance we need out there on the field. They're high school juniors and seniors, so they absolutely know this. The gym door opens and Dereck walks in.

"Time," I say.

The girls exhale as they stand upright.

"Go get water," I add.

"Is it me or does he look better than usual?" Morgan asks as they walk away giggling.

"I'm sorry I'm late," Dereck says when he reaches me.

"No biggie. I made them start their usual drills." I glance toward the window. "It looks like it's going to rain today, so we moved the equipment inside."

"The basketball team is supposed to have practice in here today." He looks at the girls, who are now running from one side of the court to the other.

"Oh crap. I didn't know." I shut my eyes and open them to look at him. "What should we do?"

"Nothing. I'll speak to Coach Dunn and see if we can turn this into a double practice. They do similar drills anyway."

As if on cue, the basketball team begins spilling through the door. The girls stop what they're doing and start talking to their friends on the team as Dereck and I head over to Coach Dunn. He's an older man that reminds me a lot of my own father, with the way he goes on and on about the weather and the grass and whatever other topic anyone places in front of him. The weather is today's topic. As I stand there quietly, my phone buzzes in my back pocket. I walk away from them and head back to where the girls are, taking my phone out of my pocket and looking at the text I have from Maverick.

Mav: Tony's tonight. 8 p.m.

I sigh heavily. Tony's is a restaurant slash bar that Maverick's sister-in-law's family owns.

Me: Aren't you sick?
Mav: I feel better
Me: That fast?
Mav: I've been sleeping all day

Me: . . .

Mav: I'll have soup

Instead of responding to him, I text Leyla and Ashley to see if they want to join us at Tony's.

Ashley: I thought Mav was sick?

Me: Apparently not.

Leyla: I'm down

Ashley: I'm out. I'm going out with Matt tonight.

Me: Ohhh. Hope it goes well

Leyla: Hit it. Hit it.

Ashley: LOL I plan to

I shake my head and laugh quietly as I put my phone away. People like Ashley are goals. She met Matt a few weeks ago at a dive bar we went to, announced he was cute, went up to him, exchanged numbers, and now they're on their third date. I feel like that should be a lesson to all of us. If you want something, go for it. Some people are like that. Unfortunately, I'm not those people. I'm too shy. Sure, I speak my mind and am blunt, but that's only if I know you and am comfortable around you. Otherwise, I'm as quiet as a mouse. Ashley says that the only reason I'm single is that I have a perpetual RBF, which automatically intimidates guys, and that even when I am interested, I don't seem to be.

For the majority of my life, I didn't care. In high school, while all of my friends were boy crazy, I wasn't. Even my own mother chalked it up to me being a late bloomer. Whatever the case was, it meant that I was officially the oldest virgin I knew and that was intimidating for sure since most people around me seemed to hook up with people without a care. The only other virgin I know is Melissa. She's beautiful, cool, confident, and has vowed to wait for marriage. Some of the girls on the team think she's crazy. I think it's commendable, but it can't be easy for her since she actually has a serious boyfriend. If my libido feels this way and I'm single, I can't even imagine what she must be going through.

With that in mind, I turn back to the girls I'm supposed to be helping coach and find Morgan poking one of the guys in the basketball team's arm. It seems that even she's mastered the art of flirting. I seriously have no hope.

Chapter Four

"I DON'T UNDERSTAND. YOU'RE FREAKING GORGEOUS, YOU'RE funny, and your body is just, I mean, I could write songs about your body."

I shoot Leyla a look. "You can't write songs to save your life, so I don't have much faith you'll do my body justice."

"See? And you know you've got it." She shakes her head. "Why are you so damn insecure when it comes to guys?"

"I'm not insecure." I frown, looking at my reflection in the mirror. "My makeup looks masterful."

"It does." Leyla nods in appreciation behind me.

"What does?" Maverick asks, walking into my room.

"Dude, you don't knock? What if we were naked?" Leyla turns to him.

"I'd ask if I could stay here and watch." He shrugs a shoulder.

"And I'd kick your ass," she says, but melts into him as he gives her a hug.

"Damn, you look . . . " He lets out a breath and shakes his head as he walks over to me. My heart speeds up.

"Right? She's getting a guy's number tonight. No, she's going home with one," Leyla says.

"Why?" Mav frowns deeply. "She doesn't need a guy to make her feel beautiful or wanted."

I roll my eyes and go back to applying my makeup. Normally, I'd agree with him, but honestly? I want to be objectified, dammit. I wouldn't say it aloud, but I want to be and feel wanted by a man. I want someone to tell me I'm hot and that they want to have sex with me, or whatever it is men tell women. I want that.

"She's going home with a guy tonight or I'll riot," Leyla says.

Maverick's brown eyes meet mine in the mirror. He looks like he wants to say something, but instead, he shrugs and starts walking out of the room again.

"I'm leaving in ten minutes, if you want a ride, be ready."

"We don't want a ride," Leyla calls out, then looks at me. "How are you going to get a guy if you hang out with them twenty-four-seven?"

"How do you get girls if you hang out with them twenty-four-seven?" I raise an eyebrow.

"Touché, however, I still stand by my original statement that women are more courageous than men and are willing to put themselves out there." She shoots me a look. "Yourself excluded, of course."

I laugh at that, because she's not wrong.

"Holy shit. Who is this vision?" Colson boasts when we get to Tony's.

"Can you stop?" I groan.

"She's trying something new," Leyla supplies.

"She wants to get a guy," Maverick adds and there's no denying the fact that he doesn't approve.

"As she should." Colson raises his beer high and eyes me up and down. "Maybe a hockey player?"

"Not you, if that's what you're getting at." I shoot him a look.

"Nope. You're right. We made a pact. No hooking up between roommates."

I fix the short dress I'm wearing as I take a seat across from Colson and Leyla and Maverick settles into the seat beside me. As they start ordering food and drinks, I take a look around the bar to see if I find anyone attractive.

"Earth to Rocky," Mav says loudly.

"What?" I meet his gaze.

"We're waiting for you to put your order in." He raises an eyebrow. "But we can wait for you to finish scouting for prey."

"Oh shut up." I laugh with an eyeroll and tell the waitress my order.

"Tequila, huh?" Mav comments after she walks away. "You must be serious about this."

"Practice is canceled tomorrow morning. Leave her alone," Leyla says across from me. "She needs to live a little."

"I do need to live a little." I smile and thank the waitress as she sets my drink down in front of me.

"And this is how you're choosing to live a little?" Mav asks.

"What is your problem? You're the one who's always telling me I need to get out more and that I'm too hyper-focused on soccer and school and whatever."

"You do need to get out more, but I didn't think you were going to take that to mean that you need to find yourself a boyfriend or a booty call or whatever it is you're looking for."

"You have booty calls all the time." I raise an eyebrow and sip my drink. "You literally just told me I need to give you pointers on that whole situation so that you can get yourself a girlfriend."

"How are you going to give him pointers?" Colson chuckles. "I think it's safe to say he dates more than you do."

"You call that dating?" I blink.

"Dating, fucking, whatever. We're too young to be tied down." Colson glances at Mav. "Don't tell me you want to be tied down, dude. Is this because your brothers are settling down?"

"They're not settling," Mav says with a frown.

"Yeah, I wouldn't call getting together with a Canó sister settling," I say. "If anything, they're the ones who are settling."

"They are pretty hot," Colson agrees. "Mav's having fun though, aren't you?"

"It gets old," Maverick says. "Before you know it, I'm going pro too and who am I going to share that with? More women who don't really care about me?"

"They take care of your stick though," Leyla says with a laugh.

"It gets old," Maverick repeats.

I wouldn't know. Unlike Maverick, who literally looks at a girl and melts her panties, this is difficult for me. Leyla's right. Hanging out with him and Colson isn't helping my cause. No one with sense is actually going to come up and hit on me when I'm sitting beside two beast hockey players. They have reputations for being party animals and having short fuses. Two things that don't necessarily make it so that other guys our age feel comfortable. Our food arrives and we all dig in quickly.

"What about an older man?" I ask.

"Like a sugar daddy?" Colson pulls a face. "Come on, Rocky. No."

"Men are dumb and immature at every age," Maverick adds. "What's the point of going for someone with more baggage?"

"He has a point." Leyla points a French fry at Mav.

"Want to switch plates?" Mav asks me after a few seconds.

I glance over at his. He got the lasagna. I got the spicy pasta primavera, but I can't eat all of this right now. Eating and consuming alcohol at the same time isn't my strong suit. Because he barely has any lasagna left, I agree to switch plates.

"Why don't the two of you date?" Leyla asks pointing a fry between the two of us. "You already act like a couple."

"Yeah right." I snort and focus on the lasagna in front of me, hoping no one notices my sudden discomfort.

"Rocky's like a sister to me," Maverick says. "That would be weird."

Fuck. There it is. The knife in my heart that I wasn't expecting but also doesn't surprise me. He friend-zoned me in just six words and it hurts more than I care to admit.

After dinner, we stick around, ordering more drinks. Normally, this is when I go home. I always have to be up at the crack of dawn for practice, but since that's been canceled, I figure I'll give myself a rest day. Besides, Tony's has live music tonight and I never get to catch the local bands that come in. There's a DJ setting up who has already started playing popular hip-hop music. Soon, the tables start emptying out and are cleared away, leaving people standing in an area that has a dance floor type of vibe. There are people dancing, but not a ton. I say this to Leyla who glances over at me with a laugh.

"Not yet. Let them get another drink in their system though." She looks over to the dance floor. "The guy in the pink shirt is absolutely going to start dancing soon."

I laugh, finding him quickly. He's already swaying from

side to side and bobbing his head as he raps along to the music. I'm not sure he needs another drink at all. A few guys come over to our table and based on their build and loudness I assume they're on the hockey team with Col and Mav. I know a lot of their teammates, but not all. They only invite a handful of them over to play video games and hang out randomly throughout the week and weekend. I'm not sure what the requirement for the invitation is. I also haven't been to many of their games since I'm always so busy with my own.

"That's Rocky." Leyla's voice cuts through my daydream and I blink up at her. She shoots me a stern look. "This is Brian and that's Chase."

"Oh. Hi." I smile at the two guys who are standing at the head of the table. Unlike Colson and Maverick, who look like a tattooed GI Joe and his badass friend, Brian and Chase look like literal Ken dolls.

"Hi." Brian does a gesture with his hand that's a sort of wave, but he makes it look cool. His piercing blue eyes stay on mine and I feel my cheeks warm. "You're the roommate."

"I am." My smile grows.

"No wonder they don't invite us over." Chase nudges Brian.

"I guess we'll have to invite ourselves," Brian says, still looking at me.

I continue to smile because I'm not sure what to say but Leyla steps in for me, saying, "Or Rocky can invite you."

"Yep." I nod, letting out a laugh.

Brian chuckles. He looks at Maverick. "Where have you been hiding this one?"

"Careful," Maverick says, jaw twitching.

"I thought you were with Madison." Brian's eyes narrow on Maverick.

"I never said that."

I look away from them and back at Leyla, shooting her a look. She hops off the high stool and slaps a hand on the table. "Keke and I will be around. It was nice to meet you guys."

At the sound of my nickname, I hop off my own chair and grab my purse. Maverick's hand closes around my wrist. My eyes snap to his and the concern I see in them instantly annoys me. Normally, I wouldn't care. It's endearing that my best friend cares about me and my well-being, but tonight is not the night. Maybe it's the tequila in my system or the fact that he called me his sister when I can't seem to stop thinking about him as more than a friend. I yank my arm away with a glare and follow Leyla.

"What the fuck was that about?" Colson asks behind me, but I ignore him.

"Girl, what was that?" Leyla asks when we get far enough away from the table. "Brian was totally flirting with you."

"I know but it was awkward with Colson and Mav there." I groan.

"It shouldn't be though." Leyla shoots me a look as we lean against the bar. "It's Maverick, isn't it? You like him."

"I might."

"You might." She laughs. "When did this happen? I thought he was your big brother and all that."

"He was. He is." I sigh. "It's a recent development. I'm still processing it."

"Well, process it whilst losing your virginity to Brian. He's walking over here right now."

"Leyla." I stand up straighter and fix my hair.

I don't know why I bothered straightening it tonight. I already feel the halo of frizz developing around my face. In typical North Carolina fashion, yesterday the weather was splendid and today the humidity is out of freaking control. I tug on the hem of the short dress I'm wearing and Leyla sets a hand on my hand.

"Stop. It's short, it's tight, but you look bomb. Stop messing with it."

"Okay." I exhale and bring the two drinks the bartender hands me over to us, giving one to Leyla, and turn around to lean my back against the bar.

"I thought I saw you two heading this way," Brian says once he reaches us. "So, what's up? What are we drinking tonight?"

"I'm having tequila," I say.

"We are drinking whatever you want to buy us," Leyla says, shooting me a look.

I sigh. I know my friends think this is the reason I'm in this predicament, but I wish they'd take a moment to hear me when I say that I don't want to get a guy to pay for my things.

It's not that I refuse for someone to buy me a drink, but I don't want it to come with a condition. I look back over to the table we vacated and see Maverick and Colson are now swamped with women. As usual. I roll my eyes and look back at Brian.

"I'm good." I shake the short glass in my hand. "I've had two, so I've reached my limit."

"That's too bad." Brian smiles. "Maybe I can take you out for a drink this weekend."

"Why not?" I shrug a shoulder and manage a smile.

"What's up?" Maverick asks. I blink up to realize he and Colson are both here now, instantly crowding our space by the bar.

"Just shooting my shot," Brian says.

"With whom?" Maverick frowns, looking around. It's sad that he doesn't even think that I'm an option.

"The hottest girl at this restaurant slash bar," Brian says, looking at Maverick like he's crazy. "Rocky."

"Oh." Mav glances in my direction and his eyes capture every single curve on my body as if he's analyzing me.

Maybe I'm imagining it, but I swear his expression heats up when he meets my eyes again. My heart flips as I hold his gaze and take a sip of tequila, hoping the liquid gives me enough courage to either look away or actually do something about this stupid crush. I push that thought away as quickly as it appears. No way in hell am I going to fall for my best friend. I've heard horror stories about that. People who lose life-long friendships because they hooked up.

"We're going on a date," Brian says.

"A date?" Maverick says, his voice a shout in the otherwise fairly quiet restaurant.

The band hasn't started playing their live music. There are conversations happening, but not loud enough to drown us out.

"Yeah, a date," Brian says. "What is up with you, dude? I have sisters. I know how to treat a lady."

At that, I smile. Brian is really handsome and obviously a decent guy. Maybe he'll be the one I finally lose my virginity to. Not that I'm in a huge rush. Okay, maybe I'm in a bit of a rush, but not enough to just sleep with whomever. I have a checklist. He has to be handsome, have nice breath, good hygiene, not burp in front of me like it's no big deal and then laugh about it, be nice but maybe not too nice. Admittedly, my list kind of sucks, but it's the only thing I know to stay away from or look for based on my limited experience. I hang out with as many guys as I do girls, but my guy friends haven't given me any indication that they're good boyfriends since the majority of them have never been in long relationships either.

Maverick dated a girl in high school, Madison, for two years. She was beautiful and smart and so nice, and he completely broke her heart when he broke up with her and they went to separate colleges. Not to say Mav wasn't hurt by it as well. He was, but he moved on pretty quickly. He started dating Monica and then Tina and then Carissa. I still follow Madison on social media and she seems really happy now, but it took her a while to get back on her feet. I could tell. According to Mav, she's been dating a guy for a little while, but they still text back and forth. I don't know what that means. Part of me thinks if given the chance, he'd get back with her in a heartbeat. I wouldn't blame him. Lord knows I would if I was in his shoes. She was a real catch. Not that I'm not, but it's obvious he doesn't see me that way, so that's a nonstarter.

I continue sipping my tequila and ignoring them as they talk about hockey and their next game and how they're going to beat Stanford.

"No way. Are you going over there or playing them here?" That's Leyla.

"We go up next Thursday," Colson says.

"So do we." Leyla grins, looking over at me. "It is next Thursday, right?"

"Yep."

"Well, shit, maybe we can hang out after the game," Brian says. "I wonder if we're sharing transportation."

"There's no better way of getting to know someone than sitting beside them on a long flight or bus ride," Leyla adds with a wink. "Trust me, I know."

"I bet you do." I laugh and finish off my drink, setting it down on the bar.

"You wanna get out of here?" she asks me. "Peyton texted about a party."

"Sure. Why not?" I shrug.

"You're just going to leave?" Mav sidles up beside me.

"You're with your boys. I'm sure you'll be fine."

"So? You always hang out with us."

"I know and I was just thinking about the fact that we need to hang out less."

"What?" He turns to me fully now, completely blocking everyone else from my vision. He really is a freaking powerhouse of a guy. "Why would we do that?"

"For starters, we already live together. We can hang out at home. And no one wants to talk to me when I'm with you, and the ones who do, you don't let." I purse my lips. "Like Brian, who had to ask me out when we were away from the table."

"Brian?" Mav chuckles. "He's not even your type."

"My type? What even is my type?"

"Well, you dated that guy Mike with the surfer dude vibe."

"Mike." I shake my head with a laugh. "We literally dated for two months. I can't believe you even remember him."

"And Danny. He was nice enough."

"Another guy I only dated for a month."

"That's your thing though." Mav shrugs. "You're a short-term dater. There's nothing wrong with that."

"A short-term dater?"

"Yeah. You date a guy, he doesn't make you happy, so you cut your losses and move on. It's smart."

"That's . . ." I shake my head. "Okay."

"What?"

"Nothing." I take a breath and start walking over to Leyla.

I've never really thought about it in those terms, probably because that's not what happens at all. What normally happens is that I start dating a guy, he wants to move way too fast, and they start acting uninterested. Sometimes they break up with me, other times I cut it off before they get a chance to. It's never a case of me moving on because they don't make me happy.

"How are you going to give me lessons in what girls want if we don't hang out?"

"You clearly do not need my help in that department."

"We can help each other."

I laugh. "How would you help me?"

"I can tell you what guys want and you can tell me what girls want."

"Guys want sex. Easy."

"Some guys want more than just sex." He says this with the most serious expression on his face.

"That's all you and Colson ever want."

"Because I haven't met the right girl."

"What about Rebecca?" I raise an eyebrow.

"Well, maybe I've met the right girl but haven't made my move yet." He sighs heavily. "I need to know what I'm doing wrong."

"For starters, you're not asking anyone out on actual dates. You're just taking them home and fucking them and then ghosting them. I can't imagine anyone would take you seriously after that treatment."

"Fair." He flinches. "That's why I need help."

"Stop taking girls home that you don't think have potential." I shrug.

"Fine."

"Okay. That's step one." I reach up and he instantly lowers his face so I can kiss him on the cheek. "See you later."

"Be careful. Call me if you need me to go pick you up or whatever."

"Okay, Dad," Leyla says, rolling her eyes. She links her arm with mine as we walk away. "I swear he hasn't stopped looking at you tonight. It's almost like he can't fathom that you're this hot and just sitting right under his nose."

"Maverick?" I shoot her a look. "You're insane. He sees me as a little sister. Don't you see how he's acting because Brian asked me out?"

"Like a jealous man."

"Or an older brother." I raise an eyebrow.

"How would you know? You don't have an older brother."

I nod. Very true. Maverick is the closest thing I have to an older brother and he's definitely not that, at least not in my mind, at least not anymore. Freaking hormones.

Chapter Five

Maverick

"SHE IS SO HOT. I CAN'T BELIEVE YOU HAVE NEVER introduced us," Brian says. "Or maybe I can. I guess if you want a piece of that."

"Don't." I shoot him a glare that makes his eyes go wide. "Don't talk about Rocky like that. She's not a piece of anything."

She's the whole damn thing, I want to say, but don't. It would make me look like I'm cockblocking or interested and I'm not. I've had a crush on Rocky for as long as I can remember, but I've never let myself entertain the thought that maybe there could be more than friendship there, not because I'm not attracted to her or think she's the coolest girl in the world. I just don't want to mess with our friendship. That was a decision I made when I was fifteen years old and stick by even now. It would complicate everything. I love her parents. She loves mine. Mine loves hers. I mean, we've spent holidays together. We've gone on trips together. I've stayed over at her house and vice versa. If her father found out I was interested in his daughter in that way he'd have my head, and as much as I love Mike, I'd never disrespect him like that. Or his daughter. I can't deny that the thought of her dating one of my teammates hurts though. Brian's a cool guy, but it doesn't matter. It's Rocky. She's worth anyone's weight in gold.

"Yo." Colson hits my chest. "You wanna ride?"

"Where?"

"A party."

I look over at Brian, who's texting on his phone. "Are you coming?"

"Sure." He doesn't look up from his phone. "I'll follow you."

"Why don't we just invite them to the house?" Colson says, looking at his own phone. "It's Laura, Mel, and Kayti. They're with some other friends. We have Brian and Chase." Colson frowns and stops walking. "Did we lose Chase?"

"I don't know how the fuck anyone would lose the giant." I look around and spot Chase in the back by the bathrooms talking to a blonde, and tap Colson so he looks where I'm looking.

"Yeah, he's not leaving," Brian says. "Unless he brings her along."

"We'll meet at our place," Colson says. "I'll text you the address."

"Let me call Mitch, he might have a keg." I pull my phone out of my pocket and call my brother.

He and his friends always have an extra keg, and if they don't, they always know where to find one. He answers fast and sounds out of breath.

"I don't even wanna know," I say, shaking my head.

"What? I was running." He chuckles.

"Running. Right." I roll my eyes even though he can't see me. Mitchell is the exact person who would answer the phone when he's fucking someone without a care in the world. I know because it's happened and I still haven't gotten over it.

"Whatever. You can ask Misty if you want."

"Oh, you're with Misty? Then I know you're definitely not running."

"Fuck you."

I laugh. Misty is a girl he dated back in high school and still hasn't gotten over. With good reason. She's the three Fs: hot as fuck, smart as fuck, and funny as fuck. She's also never giving him the light of day again, apparently. He's been trying and failing to hook up with her for five years. Now they're hanging out because of some assignment or something and they're spending more time together than ever, but I can tell my brother's balls are bluer than a damn Smurf. It would be funny if I couldn't relate, living with Rocky and all. Not that Rocky leads me on. Or touches me. But sometimes, she looks at me with these bedroom eyes and I swear my heart stops beating all together.

"What do you want?" he asks, still obviously bothered.

"I need a keg."

"Or two," Colson says beside me.

"Hell no. Last time I hooked you up with a keg you destroyed that hotel room and I felt responsible."

"I paid for it."

"No, Dad paid for it."

"I paid Dad back every cent."

"How?" Mitchell sounds genuinely curious. "You don't have a job."

"You know I have side hustles."

He's quiet for a long time. "You're not selling drugs, are you?"

"What the fuck?" I stop walking for a second. "Why in the world would I be selling drugs? You want Mom to kill me or something?"

Colson laughs beside me, shaking his head. "Momma's boy."

I bring my hand up and show him my middle finger. "Can you get us the keg or not?"

"Give me fifteen minutes." Mitch sighs heavily into the phone. "This is for your house?"

"Yeah."

"You need to keep it in the yard. And not destroy that

fucking house. That's an original Craftsman home from the thirties. Mom would—"

"Mitchell, can you shut up and just get what I asked and go to my house? We're not savages."

"Right." He scoffs. "Except you kind of are."

"We will not destroy anything." I take a deep breath before I hang up the phone. "Invite Misty."

"I take it that's a yes?" Colson asks.

"Yeah, he had to give me a whole speech about not destroying anything."

"Fuck that. Your parents will kill us if anything gets destroyed. Again. We need to keep everyone in check."

"That's what happened last time," I say.

"Don't invite Reuben."

"So we can hear him bitch about it for the next week?"

"I don't care. You want Reuben in our house?"

"No."

I don't even want Brian in our house, but that's for a different reason and I refuse to go down that road.

Chapter Six

Rocky

I'M ALMOST HOME WHEN I FINALLY LOOK AT MY PHONE AND FIND a text and missed call from Maverick.

Mav: Heads up: we're having a party at the crib

"I hate when people say crib," Leyla says beside me. "What is this? The year two-thousand?"

"Stop reading my texts." I roll my eyes and put my phone away. "They're supposed to consult me before they throw parties."

"Oh, come on, Barnes, it's just one party."

"You're just saying that because you're drunk."

She sets her head against my shoulder. "Totally drunk. You should be drunk too."

"Someone needs to stay vigilant."

The Rulebreaker

"If I ever have a daughter, I want her to be like you." She sighs. "Such a good girl."

I roll my eyes, but smile. Most of the time, I hate being called a good girl. I hate being the one who never gets drunk or high or walks on the wild side. I hate being the prude and Goody-Two shoes who has virtual dates with her parents on Sundays at the movies. I didn't always hate those things about myself, but being here, where I see my friends let loose and do all of the things they won't be able to do later in life, I realize that I've been missing out on so much. The problem is, the good girl thing isn't an act and it's tough to shed. I think that's why I'm so good at soccer. I immersed myself in it from early on and leave everything out on the pitch. I exhaust myself in training, in practice, in games, so that by the time I get home, I just focus on studying and getting rest. Mom doesn't like it. She says I definitely need to live a little. Dad has always been strict, so he obviously loves the way I am.

When the Uber pulls up in front of my house, my mouth drops. Leyla picks her head up from my shoulder with a gasp.

"Oh my God," we say in unison. "What the hell?"

"I'm going to kill them," I say under my breath as I exit the Uber and hold Leyla's hand to make sure she doesn't fall.

"I'll help you," she says. "I cannot believe they didn't talk to you about this."

We stay frozen on the sidewalk, on the edge of the lawn that is always meticulously kept, thanks to the landscaper that Maverick's mom hired. The house is a huge old-school

Craftsman, with a porch and thick wood columns painted white. The house itself is a mix of gray rocks and white wooden planks. It's dreamy and right off Franklin Street, which makes it extremely coveted. Before I was accepted here, I had no idea what a gem this was, but after a year of being here, when Maverick's old roommate moved out and he asked me if I wanted to move in, I jumped at the chance.

The bars are here, the Greek life is here, every single rich parent who's an alumnus comes back for home games and has fancy barbecues on their fancy lawns. Basically, it's a dream, and it currently has at least forty people spilling out of the house and onto the lawn. If it's this crowded here, I can't imagine how it is inside or in the yard. My heart speeds up. *My room.* I grab Leyla's hand even tighter and start marching up the walkway, shouldering past people as we walk into the house. The living room is crowded, the lights are completely off, and there's a freaking DJ with a smoke machine and strobe lights. I shut my eyes for a second and try to stop the impending meltdown I feel coming on. This is Colson and Maverick's house as much as it is mine. More, really. Mav's parents own the place and are letting us live here rent-free, despite Colson and I trying to pay them. *It's not my place. I'm just happy to be here.* I repeat those things on loop and take a deep breath as I open my eyes. If they want to have a party, that's fine. It doesn't mean I have to partake.

"You good?" Leyla asks beside me.

"I'm good." I glance over at her. "Are you staying?"

"I'm tired." She yawns. "We have practice in the afternoon tomorrow."

"You can crash in my room."

"Nah. I think I'm going to grab a water bottle and head out."

"I'll walk with you." I walk beside her to the kitchen, dodging dancing guys and swaying girls.

As we walk into the kitchen, I spot Mitchell. There's a group of girls swarming around him, but he's hard to miss, with his height and wide smile. He's wearing a backward baseball cap, his wavy hair brushing against his neck. I always thought he was the hottest Cruz brother of the three, with his piercing green eyes and caramel complexion. The three of them are hot, I mean, the oldest, Jagger, is super-hot, but there's something about Mitch that always stood out to me. Even before the three of them had that crazy growth spurt in high school that shaped them into what they are today, I always thought he was the cutest one. That is, until this stupid crush on Maverick started. I beeline over to Mitch, shouldering through the girls. He lowers the beer bottle in his hand and quirks an eyebrow at me. Seriously. Hot. And another Cruz family member who only sees me as a little sister.

"Damn, Little One." Mitch eyes me up and down. "You're looking . . . not like yourself tonight. What's the occasion? Hot date?"

"No." I roll my eyes. "Where is your idiot brother?"

"Out back." Mitch chuckles, then turns serious. "Did he not run this by you?"

"He did not."

"Oh shit. I'll take you to him." Mitch walks away from the girls, not even bothering to say anything as he leads the way to his little brother. "I would tell you to go easy on him, but he needs to be held accountable for something." He chuckles.

The Cruz brothers are super close. When Jagger was still going to school here last year, before he signed an NFL contract, the three of them were inseparable. Always at dinner together, at bars, at parties. On the rare occasion they weren't together, they were still keeping up with the others' whereabouts. I'm an only child, so hanging around them is the closest I've ever gotten to having siblings, which is another reason I shouldn't be thinking about how hot either of them are. At six foot six, Maverick towers over most of the crowd. Colson is the only one who stands at his height, and he's a few feet away, his tongue down some girl's throat. Mav has a finger hooked into the belt loop of the jeans of the girl gazing up at him dreamily and he looks like he's about to meet the same fate as Colson. She's pretty, too, dark blonde hair, great body, easygoing smile. I watch as he leans down and kisses her gently. It makes my blood boil, but I try not to show it.

"Can I talk to you?" I step beside them, crossing my arms. He pulls away from the girl's mouth and looks at me, bewildered. She wipes her lower lip and takes a step back nervously.

"What's up?" Mav frowns at me, then looks at Mitchell,

The Rulebreaker

who's standing beside me with his arms also crossed. "What's going on?"

"What's going on is that we agreed, from the very beginning of this living arrangement, that we'd discuss things like this." I wave a hand around the backyard, filled with people around the keg and the white foldable table set up for beer pong.

"Yeah, which is why I texted you." He's still frowning as he turns to fully face me, the girl beside him forgotten like all the others his lips have touched. "You said you were in the mood to party, so I brought a party to you."

"You are so full of shit." I cock my head. "If you'd been thinking of me, which you weren't, you wouldn't have texted me after you probably spoke to Mitchell about bringing the keg."

"You told her I called you for a keg?" Maverick looks at his brother in disbelief.

"No." Mitch chuckles. "I didn't say anything."

"I've known you for ten years, Maverick." I grind my teeth. "I know all of your moves before you make them."

"What do you want me to do, Rocky? Everyone's here, people are having fun. I'm having fun, maybe you'd have a little fun if you'd get out of your own head once in a while. Didn't you say you wanted to meet a guy or whatever? Here. Guys." He waves an arm around.

"You know what? You're right. Is Brian here? I'd love to continue our conversation." I look around, even though I'm really not looking for Brian and just want Mav to think I am. "Didn't you say you wanted to meet someone worth settling down for?"

"I'm still waiting for you to make me that list on how to woo impossible women."

"Impossible women?" I raise an eyebrow and laugh despite myself. I can never stay mad at him too long. "Why would you want to woo an impossible woman?"

"Because possible women are easy to get." He looks at the girl still standing beside him. "No offense. Being a possible woman is a great thing, babe."

"No offense taken." She shrugs a shoulder, shaking the red cup in her hand. "I'll be back in a few minutes. I'm out of beer."

"Babe?" I shake my head. "Gross."

"Put it on the list then."

"I will."

"What list are you talking about?" Mitchell asks. "This started out as a promising argument, but like every other argument the two of you have, it became something else."

"Rocky's going to make me a list of things to do and say or not do and not say so that I can get a woman. A real woman. Not just a fuck buddy."

"You do realize all you have to do is not fuck every woman you meet and show the ones you see a future with that you're serious." Mitch's brows pull in deeper.

"You do realize I've tried that and it hasn't worked," Mav says.

"He has." I look at Mitchell. "He actually dated a really nice girl, Mauve, and he screwed it up by screwing her friend."

"I didn't know they were friends," Maverick states.

"If you're serious about someone, you don't go around screwing other people." I shoot him a look.

"Okay, Mom." Mav rolls his eyes. "So are we cool?"

"Like I said, I'm going to go find Brian."

"He's not even your type," Maverick shouts. "Seriously, Rocky, why him?"

"Why not him, Mav?" I shrug a shoulder and walk away, leaving him and his brother behind.

I'm not really planning on going to look for Brian. My plan is to go to my room and lock the door and forget this party is happening, but on my way in, I do spot Brian, and he smiles when he sees me, so I walk over to him. I don't know why Maverick thinks he's not my type. He's hot and nice and that's good enough for me.

Chapter Seven

Maverick

I'VE BEEN WATCHING ROCKY AND BRIAN FLIRT FOR WHAT FEELS like an hour. It's not like she doesn't deserve to live her life and do whatever she wants, but he's definitely not who I would have chosen for her.

"What's wrong with Brian?" Mitchell asks beside me. He's been babysitting the same beer since he got here. It has to be lukewarm by now.

"Nothing. Why?" I tear my gaze away from them and look at my brother.

"You're watching them like a hawk, so I assume something is wrong with him."

"Oh." I look at them again. Rocky's laughing so hard, she's bending forward and Brian is loving it. An uneasy feeling settles in the pit of my stomach.

"At least he makes her laugh. We all know how difficult that can be to do," Mitch says. "It's nice to see her let loose once in a while."

"Yeah."

"She looks fucking hot too," he continues. "That dress? I mean, damn."

"Gross, Mitchell. That's Rocky you're checking out." I shoot him a look.

"I didn't say I was going to do something about it. I'm just admiring how hot she looks. I don't know why she wears all those baggy clothes all the time when she has that underneath."

"Maybe she doesn't want to be objectified."

"Maybe." My brother shrugs. "Or maybe she's insecure, which would suck, considering she has the perfect body."

"Can you stop checking her out?" I push my brother's shoulder.

He stumbles a couple of steps and looks at me in disbelief. "Dude, what the hell?"

"Just . . . stop looking at her, stop talking about her, just stop."

"Holy shit." He searches my eyes. "You . . . like her?"

"No. Of course not." I scowl. "She's my best friend. What the hell is wrong with you? She's always been a little sister to you and now all of a sudden you're talking about her like she's a conquest."

Mitchell laughs. "Wait till Jagger hears about this."

"About what?" I feel my scowl deepen. "Stop trying to start shit."

"I'm not trying to start anything. I'm appreciating how she looks in that dress. You're taking it somewhere else. Newsflash, if she wore the dress it's because she wants people to notice how good she looks."

"That's not true."

"Yes, it is, bro."

I set my jaw as I think about that. I know a lot of girls are like that, but not Rocky. She's not afraid to try out a new sport and get hurt or mess up her hair when we're outdoors. She's always been that way, choosing to hang out with us rather than going to the spa or whatever. She enjoys being one of the guys. She's told me that herself. The idea that she's wearing that dress because she wants people to notice her—guys to notice her—is ridiculous. She doesn't even like it when guys hit on her whenever she goes out.

"You're still staring."

I sigh heavily. "I just can't figure her out."

"I don't think she wants you to, man." Mitch pats my shoulder. "Just let her be. We can't be overprotective forever."

"Yeah," I say distractedly because I don't mean it.

Her parents are counting on me to protect her. They made it clear that it was the reason they wanted her moving in here. I don't think they'd enjoy knowing that I'm the one she needs protecting from.

Chapter Eight

Rocky

"I LOVE YOUR NAME."

"Thank you." I smile up at Brian.

"I mean, when you first told me what it was, I almost didn't believe you, and you're so gorgeous, I wasn't sure it fit, but it does."

"Thanks." I frown. "I guess?"

"It's a compliment." He chuckles lightly, reaching for my hand. "So what are your plans for the rest of the night?"

"I don't really have any."

"Hm. You live here, right?"

"Yep." My face warms as his thumb draws circles along mine.

"Why don't you show me your room?"

"Um." I pull my hand from his and look around. "I don't

think it's a good night for that. There's a lot of people and a lot of noise."

"Which is why going to your room would be better."

"For what exactly?" I ask in a near whisper, meeting his blue eyes.

"For this." He leans in and kisses me.

It's a soft kiss, his lips tentative on mine until I open my mouth for his tongue to slide in. I reach out and grab his hair as the kiss deepens, and suddenly the music stops, the lights turn on, people groan and complain all around us, and we pull away.

"That was . . ."

"Party's over," Maverick yells. "Unless your name is Colson or Rocky, kindly get the fuck out of our house."

My eyes widen.

"I guess I better get going." Brian steps into me again, crowding the stool I'm sitting on.

"Yeah, I guess so." I swallow.

"We still on for that date?"

"Yep." I smile.

"Friday at six?"

"Can we make it seven?" I scrunch my nose. "We're playing a scrimmage on Friday and those always run late."

"Seven-thirty then."

"Perfect."

He kisses me again.

"Out," Maverick yells. "Out, out, out. GET THE FUCK OUT."

We pull away quickly. I look over at Maverick, wide-eyed. He's staring right at me with a furious expression on his face. What the hell is wrong with him?

"He obviously isn't getting laid tonight," Brian comments.

"Apparently not." I keep looking at Maverick, who's still watching me. "See you Friday then."

"See you Friday." Brian walks away.

I stay where I am for another two seconds before walking to my room. I gather my things quickly and shower. The guys let me have the master suite since it's the only one with a bathroom and they thought it would be weird if we all shared one. When they said that, I laughed it off and told them they were crazy, but I'm so glad they thought of that because they weren't wrong. After I'm dressed in my pajamas—an oversized UNC soccer shirt and cotton shorts—I exit the bathroom, turn off the lights, and sigh into my pillow. The exhaustion of the day finally catching up and sinking into my bones as I shut my eyes.

Chapter Nine

Maverick

COLSON PUSHES HIS SHOULDER INTO MINE AS WE FIGHT FOR THE puck. I nudge him harder and continue to stick-handle it and shoot it toward the goal. Russell easily blocks it and hits it back in our direction. This time, Colson gets in front of me and takes it, handling it to the back of the line where I meet him so we can start over.

"So." He exhales heavily. "That party was something before you cut it short."

"That party was lit." Reagan turns around and nods. "Gina says she wants you to throw one every week."

"Fat chance." I scowl underneath my helmet. "Unless Gina and her sorority sisters are going to help clean up the mess you left behind."

"We were guests," Reagan says.

I roll my eyes. My mother would definitely agree with him. Even when my brothers and I were little, she always made us pick up all of our toys after our friends left, despite their mothers wanting them to help us. Mom always said, if you invite people over, they're supposed to be taking a break, not contributing to your chores. This is why I opt to go to parties instead of hosting them myself. Colson and I were up till four in the morning making sure the house was picked up.

"You should've asked Rocky to help you," Reagan adds. "But according to Brian, she wasn't very happy about the party, to begin with."

I set my jaw and choose not to respond. My first instinct is to scream, "Fuck Brian," and that would be completely fucked up, especially since Brian is the nice guy on the team. The one breaking up fights at bars and encouraging us when we're losing games. I stand by what I said to Rocky. He's not her type, but that may not be a bad thing. Her type kind of sucks. They've all been nice enough, but they haven't treated her the way she deserves to be treated. Maybe Brian can change that.

"We're up," Colson says and we skate up and start doing the battle drill again; this time he has the puck and I'm the one trying to get it from him.

Brian skates past us, and I try not to think about his date with Rocky. It's not fair for me to feel like I have any kind of ownership over her. This is the kind of shit I would normally talk to her about without giving it a second thought, but I can't bring it up without sounding like a simp for her because that would send the wrong message. Yes, I think she's beautiful and hot and the coolest girl in the world. That doesn't mean I want to date her. She's my best friend. I push Colson a little harder and take the puck from him, skating away while he chases closely behind me.

"You motherfucker."

I chuckle. "You need to be quick on your feet, man."

His stick hits mine as he gets next to me again, but it's too late and he knows it. Once the puck is mine, no one can take it from me. Well, maybe Brian, and isn't that the most ironic thing? I laugh at myself as we continue with practice. I need to be ready for Monday's game and the last thing I need are distractions.

Chapter Ten

Rocky

I'M DRIBBLING THE BALL DOWN THE PITCH WHEN I HEAR THE whistle. I exhale as I come to a stop and look back at our coach, waving us over. Time out, I guess. I was completely in the zone and headed toward the goal. Dammit. I pick up the ball, toss it to the referee closest to me, and run back to my coach, joining on the huddle.

"This is a community college for Christ's sake. What the hell are you doing out there?" she says sternly, not yelling, but not quite nice either.

Coach Yolanda always knows how to get us standing a little straighter without doing or saying much. She's a strict mother goose and we all fall into place when she's around.

"I told you to play down the field. The only one following directions is Barnes and she looks like she's daydreaming out there," she continues, shooting me a look. "Don't worry, you're daydreaming and playing with heart, so whatever you're thinking about is working."

I shut my eyes as some of my teammates start to snicker. Coach Yolanda silences them with a look.

"Play it down the field. Rocky, pass the fucking ball to Ashley."

"Got it." I nod and take a breath with my hands still on my hips.

"Go, go, go. We have twenty minutes left and nothing on the board. That's embarrassing."

All of us run back out. She's not wrong. This game doesn't count, but it has been embarrassing thus far. We should have at least two on the board, one from me and one from Leyla, but both were blocked by chance at the very tips of the goalie's fingers. I look at the formation on the pitch and shake my head, pointing at Ashley and Megan so they switch places. They do and we continue on. This time, when Leyla throws the ball in from the sideline, I dribble it toward Ashley. Soon, there are two girls on me trying to take it, but I put on my invisible visor and continue on, running a little harder, until I can only see one of them beside me, her foot trying to intercept mine, and hear another breathing hard to my right. I glance over at Ashley, who's already in position. The next time the defender sticks her foot between mine and then takes it away, I kick it to Ashley, who head butts it toward the goal. We wait, breathing hard, anticipation coursing through us, and watch as the ball goes over the goalie's left shoulder. I throw my hands up and scream as I run over to Ashley, throwing my arms around her.

"That's right, baby," Leyla's shouting. "That's fucking right!"

We all laugh as we hug and get right back to playing until the game is over.

"At least we got one on the board," Leyla says after Coach Yolanda finishes giving us our after-game speech and walks out of the room.

"Thanks to Ash." I finish drinking my bottle of water with one last long chug and glance over at Ash, whose face is still redder than a tomato.

"I just wanted you to be in a good mood for your big date tonight," Ash shoots back with a wink.

I laugh as the rest of my teammates start talking about that and even though no one will know because of my complexion, I feel my face heat up as much as Ashley. I used to leave as soon as I could, but after the school spent all this money on this state of the art facility, I figure I might as well use it. After a shower and soaking in an ice tub, I grab my things and head home. When I get there, Colson and Maverick are in the kitchen eating, as usual. They both stop talking and chewing when they see me.

"Dude, what is this? Are you a model now?" Colson asks.

I roll my eyes. "I wear some tight clothes and suddenly I'm a model."

"Well, yeah. You normally walk around in baggy shit that doesn't show off your figure." Colson shrugs a shoulder. "You look really good."

"Thanks." I smile as I walk to the fridge and grab one of my prepared glass water bottles infused with lemon. When I turn around to face them, I catch Maverick checking me out, and instantly feel my heart kick into high gear.

"So, the date's tonight," he says, meeting my eyes.

"Yep. I have to go do my makeup but he should be here soon."

"Where are you guys going?"

"I don't know yet." I open the water bottle and take a sip.

"Does he know you love the movies?"

"I didn't tell him that, so unless you mentioned it, no."

"Hm." Mav keeps staring.

"What?"

"Nothing." He blinks rapidly and looks away. "Have fun on your date."

"I will. What are you guys up to tonight?"

"No good," Colson says.

"So, the usual?"

Colson smiles. Maverick is on his phone now, not paying attention. I signal a peace sign and walk out of the kitchen with my water and my feelings. If they're planning on their usual Friday night that means they'll go to a bar, pick a fight, pick up some girls, and bring them back to the house. If I'm lucky, I'll be passed out by the time they start screwing them and if I'm really lucky I won't be here in the morning to deal with the walks of shame, but I have the worst luck when it comes to that so I'm not holding my breath.

Chapter Eleven

"This is good," Brian says to the waitress as she sits us in a booth near the windows.

"This is nice." I smile as I look around. It's probably the fanciest restaurant I've ever been to while I've been here. Not that I've been to many regular restaurants at all while I've been here. Or dates for that matter.

"I'm glad you like it. I hear the lasagna is great."

"I guess we'll find out."

Brian smiles. "Do you drink wine?"

"Not particularly, but I'll have some if you're having some."

"I was thinking we could order a bottle." He looks at the wine list.

"That's very . . . grown-up. I'm down to share a bottle."

"It does feel very grown-up, doesn't it?" He chuckles. "My mom likes dry red wines, so she kind of put me onto those."

"That's cute, so you drink wine with your mom?"

"When I'm home I do." He glances up at me. "She was the one who told me about this place. UNC is my parents' alma matter, so they drive over whenever there's a big game."

"Drive over from where?"

"Wilmington."

"Is that home for you then?"

"Yep." He smiles wide. "I'm a Carolina boy through and through."

"I can see that." I smile back. "What do your parents do?"

"They're both chiropractors and have their own practice."

"That's very cool. My parents are nurses."

"That's awesome. I guess our parents chose careers that'll never go out of business."

"Yep. What are you planning on doing after you graduate?"

"Become a chiropractor." Brian chuckles. "I have four more years of school ahead of me. What about you?"

"I'm going to play in the National Women's Soccer League."

"Really?" He raises an eyebrow and looks at the waitress when she comes by to ask for our drink order. He orders wine for us and we put in our food order since we both know we're getting the lasagna. When she walks away, he looks at me again. "So, professional soccer."

"It's the only thing I've ever wanted. I figure if it doesn't work out for me, I can always go to nursing school and follow in my parents' footsteps, but I won't be able to try out for teams in ten years."

"I'm sure you would be able to." He frowns.

"I mean, sure, you have Pearce and Formiga who both competed in their forties, but it's not the same. You play hockey, you know how it is. You give your life to a sport and your body starts to slow down at some point."

"You make a good point."

We continue talking about our plans for the future and find that we have a lot in common. After dinner, I'm feeling full, a little buzzed, and grateful when Brian pays for dinner, so when he asks me if I want to keep the night going and go to a bar where his friends are hanging out, I immediately agree. The bar is only a block down from the restaurant, on Franklin Street, so we decide to walk over there, pushing through the now crowded sidewalks. When we get to the bar, we hand over our IDs for the bouncer to check and Brian makes small talk with him as we walk inside.

"I take it you come here often," I say over the loud music.

"Every weekend." He smiles, nodding toward the back of the bar. "The guys are over there. Can I get you anything?"

"Just water."

"Water?" He blinks at me. "On a Friday night?"

"I have to be up early for training, so yeah." I smile sheepishly.

"Ah, I didn't know you had practice tomorrow. We could've rescheduled this for tomorrow night."

"No biggie. I kind of train every morning, so it wouldn't have mattered."

"Seven days a week?" He gawks at me. "I guess this is why you're going pro and I'm not."

I laugh as we reach the bar and he leans against it. I look over at the group of guys he pointed at earlier and notice they've taken over two booths and the standing room near the bar. That's when I spot Maverick and my stomach does a little flip. He hasn't seen me. He can't, with the way his tongue is down the girl on his lap's throat. I don't miss the way his hand grazes over her chest, or the way she has a knee pressed up against his jeans, where he's surely hiding a hard-on. The scene does something to me. I'm suddenly hot and cold at the same time. Angry and turned on. This is my best friend, for goodness' sake. I really don't want to feel this way around him or about him. I excuse myself and head straight to the back of the bar, in search of a bathroom. Once inside, I shut myself in a stall and press my back against the door, closing my eyes, willing my body to stop reacting to what I saw out there. Maybe I should leave. Maybe I should call it a night right this second, call Leyla or Ashley or Rea, or any one of my teammates to ask them if they'd let me crash at their place. I decide to go that route and take out my phone to text Leyla and Ashley first. They're roommates, so surely one of them will answer quickly.

Once that's settled, I exit the bathroom and rejoin Brian. He smiles when he sees me, then stops smiling when he takes a good look at my face.

"What's going on?"

"I don't feel so well," I say quietly in his ear.

It's not a total lie. I don't feel well being here. I chance a glance in Maverick's direction and see that even though he's still firmly grabbing onto the girl's ass, he's no longer making out with her. With the way he's looking at her, like she's the only person worthy of his attention, it doesn't matter. My heart feels like it's being stabbed repeatedly at the sight of it either way.

"You want me to take you home?"

"No, it's okay. You should stay. You just got a drink and your friends are here."

"You sure?" His brows pull together slightly and I can tell if I ask him to accompany me, he would.

"Positive." I plaster the biggest smile on my face.

After a quick hug, I leave the bar and step into the Uber waiting for me outside. I could walk the few blocks home, but I'd never hear the end of it, not from my parents or Maverick. The driver and I small talk during the four minutes it takes for her to drop me off at the front of my house. I was going to Ashley and Layla's, but changed my mind at the last minute. Once inside, I shut the door and take a breather. It's quiet in here, the way it often is on weekends. I'm pulling my pajamas over my head when I hear my phone buzz and walk over to see a text from Mav.

Mav: *Where are you?*

I frown, and shoot back, *Home. Why?*

Mav: *I just saw Brian and he said you left. Why didn't you let him take you home? Did you walk?*

Me: *I Ubered. I was fine.*

Mav: *You should've told me. I would've gone with you.*

I sigh heavily and plop down on the bed as I type, *You were busy.*

Mav: *???*

Me: *You had your tongue down that girl's throat.*

I see the three dots appear, disappear, and appear again as he types out a response. I'm not sure why I'm so invested in this conversation, to begin with, considering he's obviously still at the bar and that girl is probably still sitting on his lap.

Mav: *You still should've told me. I would've gone with you.*

I stare at his response. I know Maverick better than anyone. I know he would have brought me home if I'd asked or told him, but what was I supposed to say? I was upset and turned on because of him and that was the reason I bailed on my date? I seriously need to get over him ASAP. Instead of responding, I set my phone on airplane mode, lock my door, and go to sleep.

Chapter Twelve

I KICK THE BALL INTO THE GOAL, TAKE A BREATH, AND RUN BACK to the first cone I set up. It's part of my Saturday morning drill. While some of my teammates are still sleeping their hangovers away, I'm out here practicing. Sometimes some of them join me, but today it's just me out here by myself, and I prefer it this way, with my rap music blasting in my ears as I concentrate on nothing else except dodging my invisible opponents, which I set up as cones for the time being, and kicking that ball into the goal. I'm on my third cone when I spot Maverick walking down the field over to me. Sometimes he joins as well. Not often though, especially not during the season when he'd rather be on the ice than out here. I don't pause on the fourth cone or the fifth; I concentrate until I get to the last cone and then I kick. Breathing heavily, I pull an AirPod out of my right ear, pausing the Drake music that was just playing, and dribble the ball back up the field as I look over at Maverick who's now standing between me and the first cone. I know he's going to try to block me if I go right before he even makes the move. It's his go-to—to go right instead of left. He always assumes his opponent will go that way to try to fake him out.

"I'm surprised you're not sleeping." I ease past him with the ball still at my feet and stop when I get to the cone.

"I hate when you get past me," he says.

"Try harder and stop making the same move over and over." I shrug a shoulder. He frowns.

"I don't always make that move. Sometimes I go left."

"How often would you say you go left?" I bring an arm up to wipe the sweat off my face. "I feel like we have this conversation every time."

He shakes his head, still frowning, and meets my eyes. "You locked your door."

"I'm surprised you came to my room at all." I fight the blush. Thankfully, I'm already hot and sweating out here so it's not like he'd know the difference.

"I couldn't sleep."

"Hm. Even after Rebecca from chemistry left?"

"I didn't bring Rebecca home."

"Right. She's the one you're holding out for."

We used to talk about this so easily, and now it makes me uncomfortable. I hate it. He's been talking about this girl for a year now and saying how she's his dream girl, perfection, the one he's going to get serious about as soon as he stops messing around, because that's what he's doing right now, getting all of this out of his system so when he settles down with Rebecca it'll be for good.

"I kissed her last night." He moves forward and snaps the ball from where it is in front of me and sets a foot over it so that it stays put until he's ready to go.

"I saw, remember?"

"Right." He smiles, not fully, but enough that I know he's remembering whatever transpired last night.

"So why are you here? Why didn't you take her home?"

"I don't know." He exhales. "It's like I'm lost on what to do, you know? It's easy to just hook up with girls but getting serious with one is another ball game. I asked her out on a date and now I don't even know how to act."

"Hm." My heart slams against my chest. I swallow down the uneasiness and look away, my gaze on the rustling leaves of the trees a few feet away. "You're interrupting my practice."

"I thought you were going to teach me the rules of engagement or whatever. I have to get this right."

"I'm sure she'll appreciate anything you do."

"Should I get her flowers?"

I sigh heavily, jog forward, and kick the ball from underneath his foot. He recovers quickly, getting it back and dribbling it up the field as I run beside him. He slows down for my benefit. If he really wanted, he'd already be at the goal scoring, but that's not what Mav comes here for. He enjoys the hustle, he's patient and persistent. It's what makes him a great striker in his own sport. We run drills like this until we're both drenched in sweat and decide we need a break. Then, we lie on the grass to catch our breath.

"It feels good out today," he says.

"It does. I was afraid it might rain." I roll my head to look at him. "So, when's the date with Rebecca?"

"Tonight."

"Damn. Okay." I swallow. I need to stop with the foolishness of letting this make me jealous and be happy for him. "So, flowers. Definitely not red roses."

"Why not?" He chuckles. "Don't red roses mean love?"

"Exactly. Are you in love with her?"

"Well, no." He frowns slightly. "I don't think anyone who gives red roses on the first date is necessarily in love."

"Well, then, they shouldn't give red roses." I look back up at the sky. "Maybe something fun and bright. She's all bubbly and shit. She'd love something bright."

"You say it like it's a bad thing." He laughs.

"It's not. I just can't relate to always being that happy."

"She's nice, right? You like her."

"I'm not the one taking her on a date." I look over at him again. "I don't have to like her."

"You're my best friend. You know I'm not going to settle down with someone you don't like."

I tear my gaze away again, trying to rein in the emotions clawing at my chest.

"What's next on the list of things to do?"

"Open the door for her." I close my eyes as I speak. "Hold her hand if it feels right."

"Did Brian hold your hand last night?"

I let out a laugh. "He did not. I think he tried and I kind of ruined it by reaching for my phone like an idiot."

"You weren't feeling it."

"I didn't say that." I open my eyes and look at him again. He's lying on his side, head propped on his hand as he watches me.

"You didn't have to. You didn't let him hold your hand, you left early. He said you didn't feel well."

"I didn't."

"Maybe you just weren't feeling it and wanted to go home." He searches my face. "Are you going out with him again?"

"I don't know." I lie on my side and prop my head on my hand as I face him. "I think he'll ask me out again. Things went well."

"So, a second date."

"Why do you say it like that?" I laugh. "You make it sound like it's the worst thing in the world."

"He's a good guy." Mav sits up suddenly, bringing his knees in and setting his arms over them. He's so damn tall he looks hilarious in that position.

"He is. Very nice. A true southern boy." I smile, sitting up to mimic his stance again.

"You do like southern boys."

"They're usually really well mannered." I purse my lips. "I mean, Ray was. Everyone else I've dated was from New York."

"True."

"Daylilies," I say after a moment. "Those are pretty flowers. They come in red."

"Would you like daylilies?" Mav meets my eyes again and for a moment I feel like he's asking me because he's going to give them to me and not her, but it's a fleeting moment because I know the truth.

I nod anyway even though I can't bring myself to speak. The truth is, I'd like anything he'd give me.

Chapter Thirteen

"I'M JUST GOING TO SEE IF I CAN STAY WITH LEYLA FOR A FEW days."

"Why?"

"Because I want some girl time."

My mother laughs in my ear. I shut my eyes to relish it. "Honey, you're with those girls twenty-four-seven. I thought they were driving you crazy."

"Yeah, well." I bite my lip.

"Did something happen with the boys?"

"No, of course not."

"You sure? Should I call Maverick myself and ask him?"

"Oh my God. No, Mom!"

She's quiet for a beat, then another. "Have you two finally realized you like each other?"

"What?" I don't mean to shout, but it's exactly what comes out of my mouth. "What are you talking about?"

"Oh, Rocky." She laughs loudly, the sound ringing through the phone line. Normally, it would warm my heart, but this feels like an attack. "You know, we and the Cruzes have a bet going to see how long it takes you two to realize it and who realizes it first."

"What?" I slap a hand over my face. I'm so glad I'm sitting in a parked car because surely this is not a safe conversation to have while driving. "What are you talking about, Mom?"

"You heard me. So, who realized it first?"

"Jesus," I mutter. "This is mortifying. Ms. Mildred is in on this little bet too?"

"Ms. Mildred started the bet, honey."

"Oh my God." I sink deeper into my seat. "This is so embarrassing."

"What's embarrassing?" She laughs.

"Mom, this isn't even funny. You're literally betting on your own daughter's emotions. This is a traumatic experience."

"Lord. Traumatic. Get over yourself, Rocky, and when you're done getting over yourself, spill the details."

I squeeze my eyes shut. "I like him but he doesn't know and before you say anything, no, he absolutely doesn't like me back."

"Yeah, right." She huffs. "Of course, he likes you back. He's not blind or stupid."

"Newsflash, he doesn't need to be blind or stupid to not like me back. Maybe I'm not his type."

"Maverick's? Are we talking about the same guy? Because all he does when he's around you is stare at you when you're not looking."

"That's such a lie."

"Who was the girl he was dating? The dark one with the big ass?"

"Tanya?"

"Yeah, well, Milly says the reason Tanya broke up with him is because she knew he liked you and she couldn't deal with it."

"Tanya broke up with him because she wanted him to take her to prom and he didn't want to." I roll my eyes.

"Right, and who did he take to prom?"

I bite my tongue.

"Who'd he take, Rocky?"

"Me, but that was because I didn't have a date and he felt bad for me."

"Really? That's the hill you wanna die on?"

My eyes pop open and I sit up straight. "I don't want to die on any hill. I'm just telling you the facts."

"The facts." Mom laughs again. "Yeah, okay, you let me know how you like it on that hill."

"Mom," I groan. "Please don't tell anyone about this, especially not Dad."

"I definitely will not be telling your father. He'll make you move out of that house in a heartbeat."

My eyes widen. I hadn't even considered that. My parents aren't extremely strict, but my father is definitely the stricter out of the two. He's a guest pastor at our church on weekends and definitely had more than a few serious talks with me about saving myself for marriage, something my mother is completely tickled by since they had me out of wedlock. Still, my dad's my dad, and as it is, my living with two guys is something he doesn't comprehend. Adding love to the equation would be the ultimate no-no, even if it is with Maverick, whom he adores.

"Well, darling, I personally think you should go home and tell him how you feel. Otherwise, you'll be subjected to watching him date other women for the rest of your lives."

"Yeah, because he doesn't like me."

"I'm never wrong about these things. Besides, Milly is his mother and you know how protective of him she is, so if even she knows he likes you, you know it's real."

With a groan, I say goodbye to my mother and hang up the phone. I already packed my bag for Leyla's before I even asked her or Ashley if I could stay over. They won't care. It's not like they haven't crashed at my place a million times, but as I get out of my car and walk up the stairs to their second-floor apartment, I'm replaying my mother's words in my head. Maverick doesn't like me. She's definitely wrong about that. I know him. If he did, I'd know. Sure, he looks at me and watches me, but he does that to everyone. Mav is the guy at the bar where if he doesn't have his tongue down anyone's throat, he's lost in deep thinking. He's an old soul. I used to make fun of him about that until I realized how similar we were. I knock on the door and wait. When Leyla opens it, she looks at me, looks at my duffel bag, then looks back up at me.

"Do we have an away game I don't know about?"

"Nope. I was wondering if I could stay here tonight. And maybe tomorrow."

"What?" She frowns, holding the door open for me to walk in. She shuts it behind me and faces me. "What's going on? Did something happen with Mav and Col?"

"No, they're fine. I just need a break."

"From Maverick?" Leyla's frown deepens.

"Oh my God. Yes, from Maverick." I let out a breath. "Why's that so hard to believe?"

"Well, you guys are like attached at the hip, Barnes."

"Do you think I can stay here?"

"Of course. You know we always have room for you."

"Thanks." I set down the duffel bag beside the couch. "Where's Ash?"

"I think she stayed at Trey's house."

"The basketball player?"

"Yep."

"Oh. Wow." I feel my eyebrows rise. "What happened to Matt?"

"Who knows."

"So, I guess the Trey thing is on again?"

"It's Ashley. She was a full-on vegan last week and went to Outback and ordered a steak two days ago. Who knows what goes on in that girl's head?"

I laugh because that is definitely Ashley, and spend the rest of the day with my bestie.

Chapter Fourteen

WHERE ARE YOU?

I stare at the text from Maverick for a second before I respond, *Staying at Leyla's tonight.*

I'm not at Leyla's right now. She dragged me out to a frat party and I'm currently waiting for none other than Brian, who happens to be part of this fraternity, to bring me a drink.

Maverick sends a slew of question marks, *?????*

Me: Girls' night

Mav: I thought you didn't like girls' night

Me: Sometimes they're necessary

Mav: So you're not coming home?

Me: Nope

Mav: Okay. I'll tell Colson

I roll my eyes because we both know Colson doesn't

give a fuck where I am, but whatever. Then I type, *Have fun on your date with Rebecca.*

Mav: *Thanks. I kind of wanted your input on what I'm wearing*

My heart drops and I hate that it does because of course he'd ask me for advice on what he's wearing. Even though his style is on point, he likes to stand in front of the mirror for the longest time. Finally, I type, *What are you wearing?*

Without warning, my phone starts buzzing with a FaceTime call. I look around to make sure I can answer, not because I'm expecting him to be half-naked or anything, but because I absolutely hate FaceTiming in public. Thankfully, I'm in a quiet area of the yard, where I can see the back door but not deal with the ruckus. I answer the phone. Maverick is smiling, but it disappears quickly.

"What is that on your head?" He frowns. "I thought you were at Leyla's."

"I'm staying at Leyla's. I'm currently at a party and this is a flower crown, thanks for noticing."

He gives me a once-over. "You look like you're naked."

"I'm wearing a tube top." I laugh.

"What the hell is a tube top?"

With a sigh, I stand up and point the phone down so that he can fully see me. I'm wearing a short beige tube top that shows off my midriff and bell bottom jeans. It's a hippie party. I also have circular sunglasses in my hand but I opt not to show those to him. I adjust the back of my jeans as I sit back down and hold the phone in front of my face again. Maverick is oddly quiet, so I search his face for some kind of sign of what he's thinking. Normally, it's easy for me to read him. Lately, not so much, and I don't know if it's because we're drifting apart or because I have feelings for him and am looking for other signs on his face. Either way, I don't like it. The thought of us drifting apart feels like a hole in my chest. We're supposed to walk each other's weddings, not be strangers when one of us gets to the altar. Which is yet another reason I need to push all of this away.

"So, what are you wearing?" I ask, taking in the black polo.

"This with jeans." He turns the camera so that it's pointing at the full-length mirror in my bedroom.

"Nice to see you're making good use of my things." I laugh.

"It's the only full-length mirror in the house."

"True." I look at him in the mirror. He always looks gorgeous, with his incredible physique and tanned skin. His curls are damp from a shower and his brown eyes are on the mirror as he looks at what he's wearing—a black polo, black jeans, and checkered Converse. "What are your other options?"

"These jeans and shoes with the Jimi Hendrix shirt you got me for Christmas."

The Rulebreaker

"Where are you going?"

"Probably a brewery."

"So, you can go with either one." I shrug a shoulder.

"I know that but I want you to pick for me." He turns the camera back to his face. "If we were going on a date to a brewery, which would you want me to be wearing?"

My heart flips. "We're not going on a date."

"I said if," he says, "like if we hadn't been friends our entire lives and I'd just met you and asked you out."

"Oh." The word comes out a whisper. What would that reality be like? I decide to ask, because why not continue to ruin this friendship? "If we'd just met for the first time, do you think you'd ask me out?"

"Absolutely." He lets out a laugh. He didn't hesitate though.

"Cool."

"Cool?" He laughs again. "So, which one?"

"I think the black polo. It's more serious but still casual because of your sneakers."

"Okay. Thanks." He grins.

"I have to go." I look up and see Brian walking toward me.

"Why? Leyla's coming to look for you so that you'll actually join the fun?"

I let out a laugh. "Not exactly."

"We only had beer. I got you a lager." Brian hands me the bottle. "I hope that's okay."

"I'm sure it's fine." I smile wide, then look at the phone again. "Okay, have fun."

"Oh, sorry, I didn't know you were on a call," Brian says.

"Is that . . . " Maverick is frowning, but I hang up on him before he can finish the sentence.

"Cheers." Brian taps his glass bottle against mine as he takes a seat beside me.

"Cheers." I smile as I take a sip. "So, this is where you hang out? It's pretty nice."

"It's really nice." He nods as he looks around the large yard where there are people playing beer pong, drinking from beer funnels, and playing cornhole. "The guys definitely make the most of it, as you can see."

"Are you close to all of them?"

"Most of them. I guess I'm closer to the ones I live with. I mean, they're my brothers. I'm an only child, so this is a dream for me."

"Living with a ton of guys is a dream?" I smile as I look over at him, but I know what he means. I'm not in a sorority, but to me, my teammates are my sisters, so I get it. As an only child, having teammates around me my entire life has definitely helped.

"It sounds weird, but yes." He chuckles.

"I get it. I can relate."

"Do you want to join the fun?" He nods over to the

people on the lawn. "Or would you rather just stay over here?"

"We can join. Who knows where Leyla is anyway?" I stand up and he follows suit.

As we walk, he holds my hand, and it feels good around mine.

Chapter Fifteen

Maverick

"You seem distracted."

"Nah, I'm here." I glance over at Rebecca and flash her a smile. "I hope you like sushi and beer, that's what I have planned for the night."

"I love both and I love this place." She walks inside the restaurant as I hold the door open for her.

"Maverick Cruz," the hostess says, blushing and smiling. "Hi. Welcome."

"Thank you." I smile back at her.

"Norma. I'm in your algebra class. I sit behind you sometimes."

"Oh. Cool." I keep smiling. I've never seen this girl in my life, but I'll take her word for it.

"Wow, she was totally checking you out," Rebecca says once we're seated.

"Who?" I pick up my menu from the table and start scrolling through it.

"The hostess. Norma."

"Oh. I didn't notice." I go back to the menu, trying to look for the roll Rocky normally gets, but I can't remember the name, and I definitely can't text her while I'm out with Rebecca and she's with Brian. I inwardly groan. Fucking Brian, of all people. Of course, she'd choose a pretty boy to go out with, even after I told her he's not her type. What do I know though, right? Maybe he is her type after all. She hasn't had a boyfriend in a while.

"You seem distracted."

"Just trying to figure out what I feel like eating." I glance up at Rebecca. "What do you like?"

"I like the Spider Roll."

"Oh, that's the one Rocky likes!" I smile and nod as I look back at the menu.

"Rocky's that girl you're always with?"

"Yeah."

"I thought you two were dating. I mean, before you finally asked me out, I figured you were dating."

"Rocky and me?" I chuckle. "No way. I've known her since we were kids."

"Maybe that's why you even walk the same."

"What?" I laugh as I lower the menu. "What are you talking about?"

"You walk the same. I swear." Rebecca laughs. Damn, she has a great laugh.

"That's so strange. No one's ever said that before."

"So, you guys are like really tight then."

"Yup."

"How does that fare in your relationships?"

"Wow. You get deep quick." I blink. "I don't think it makes a difference in our relationships."

"No? Your past girlfriends haven't been jealous of your friendship?"

"I mean, I haven't had a girlfriend in a while." I shrug a shoulder.

"How long?"

"Since high school."

"Oh. And why'd you break up?"

"College." I let out a laugh. "I don't think anyone has grilled me this hard on a first date."

"Well, they should." She smiles.

We pause the conversation to order our food and then she goes right back to grilling me. I don't know how I feel about it. I don't hate it. I've been waiting to go out with this girl far too long to care what she wants to talk about and I'm thinking if she's this into my personal life, it's definitely a good sign. My mind keeps drifting to Rocky though. Maybe because Rebecca has brought her up so much. Maybe because she just informed me that we walk the same, which is wild. My parents walk the same. They even share the same mannerisms, but they've been together since they were teenagers and married for thirty years, so it makes sense.

"What about you? I bet you've had a lot of boyfriends," I say.

"Not a lot. I am a serial dater though. At least that's what my friends say." She laughs.

"A serial dater." I raise an eyebrow. "So, you've dated a lot of guys while you've been here?"

"Not a lot. I mean, I go on a lot of dates, but none have turned into anything serious."

Interesting. I don't really have anything to say to that, so I sip on my lemon water instead. I don't know why I figured Rebecca was this put-together girl who had everything figured out. Like Rocky. Fuck. Why the hell am I thinking about Rocky again?

"You seem distracted again."

"I'm not. I'm good. I'm just . . . " I exhale heavily. "Yeah, I'm distracted. I'm sorry."

"What are you thinking about?"

"Nothing of importance." It's a lie, but what am I supposed to say? There's no right answer to that question.

"Hm." She glances away and I know I've upset her and it doesn't take a rocket scientist to figure out why.

I've spent an entire year pining after this girl and finally have her sitting in front of me only to not even be interested in having a conversation with her. I'm annoyed with myself. The food comes quickly and we start eating. Soon, we're making small talk, a far cry from all the relationship questions she was trying to get me to answer earlier. Maybe I'm acting this way because I haven't been on a date in such a long time. Maybe I'm acting this way because I know Rocky is with Brian and for some crazy reason I don't like that thought. Either way, I need to snap out of it.

I tossed and turned all night and finally gave up on sleep an hour ago. I went for a run, worked out, and now, I'm freshly showered and dressed. I look at the time and pick up my phone to call my mom before she heads into church.

She answers on the first ring. "Mav? Is everything okay?"

"Yeah." I frown. "Why?"

"It's before noon on a Sunday. You normally don't call this early."

"I know." I take a gulp of water and sigh heavily as I set it down. "Rocky's staying with her friend this weekend."

"Okay?" My mother's voice is understandably confused.

"This entire weekend. She just packed up and left."

"Is that unusual?"

"Yeah. I mean, she's never done it before." I pick up the water again.

"You miss her so much that you decided to wake up early on a Sunday and call me to tell me about it when you know I'm on my way to church?"

I set the cup down. "No. I mean, I guess."

"Are you telling me you have feelings for her?"

"No." My voice is louder now. "I'm just telling you what's going on in the house."

"And you don't have feelings for her?"

"I . . . " I feel myself frown. "I was on a date last night."

"And how did that go?" My mother sounds like she's one second away from telling me to fuck off, but I know she won't, so I continue on.

"It was fine. It was with Rebecca. The girl from—"

"Yes, yes, I know who it is. You've been talking about her all year."

"Well, yeah. So, it was good."

"Good enough that you obviously didn't take her home with you and woke up thinking about your best friend instead?"

"Mom."

"Maverick, I'm your mother, not an idiot." She sighs. "Look, I'm about to be late for church, so I'll make this quick. You have feelings for Rocky. If you don't see that, you need to take a good look at yourself and re-evaluate what you think you feel. If you like her, tell her."

"If I like her and I tell her I'll drive her away."

"You'd be surprised."

That gives me pause. "Mike would kill me."

"That's what you're worried about? Her father?" Mom laughs. "You're too much."

"I just . . . he's not even completely sold on the idea of her living with me."

"I wonder why."

I open my mouth and shut it a few times.

"Goodbye, Maverick. I love you. I'll pray for you."

I laugh. "Love you, Mami."

She hangs up and I stand there, staring at the cup of water in front of me. I love Rocky, but she's my best friend. If I lose her friendship, what will I really be left with? I decide this is probably a better subject to talk to my brothers about. I love my mom, but what does she know about relationships? She's been married to the same person for like thirty years. I look at the time again. Nine-thirty. Jagger's definitely awake, but he has a game today, and I'm not going to be the reason my professional football-playing brother is distracted, so I'm definitely not calling him. Mitchell is definitely not awake yet. Not on a Sunday. It's really the only day we sleep in. Except for me, apparently, today. I need to keep busy and not call Rocky just yet. She's always my go-to when it comes to things. Unfortunately, I can't really talk to her about this without disclosing my feelings and I don't think I can do that just yet.

Chapter Sixteen

Rocky

I SHOOT THE CRUMPLED NAPKIN INTO THE WASTEBASKET AND WAIT to make sure I made it in before turning and walking toward the theatre. I already spoke to my parents, who are also getting ready to watch *Mortal Kombat*. This was definitely not my first choice, but Dad was really excited about it when he saw the trailer, and Mom and I went along with it because we're usually the ones picking the movies and Dad never complains about it. My phone buzzes just as I sit down in the top middle row. The good thing about catching a movie right when they open on a Sunday is that the only people who are there are parents with small children and me and a lot of the time it's just me. I pull out my phone and see a text from Maverick.

Mav: What movie are you watching?

I frown, then type, *Mortal Kombat. What are you doing up?*

Mav: *What theatre? Number 2 or 4?*

Me: *2. Are you here?*

I wait for a response, but it doesn't come. Instead, I see a really tall guy wearing a backward baseball cap walk in and head up the stairs until he reaches my row.

"What are you doing here?"

"Watching Mortal Kombat."

"You hate the movies."

"I like popcorn." He shrugs a shoulder and sits beside me. He has a huge bucket of popcorn in one hand and a matching soda cup.

"You don't even drink soda."

"It's water in a big-ass cup."

"Oh." I frown. "I hope you didn't pay for that."

"Are drinks free?" He sets it in the cupholder opposite of me.

"When it's water from the machine."

"Damn."

I shake my head because *how does he not know that?* The lights dim low and the previews start playing. I stretch out my legs as Maverick fiddles with his seat, setting it to recline like mine.

"Who picked Mortal Kombat?"

"Are you seriously going to talk during previews?" I glance over.

"It's just previews. It's not the actual movie."

"I think I know what previews are, Mav." I roll my eyes. "How am I supposed to know whether or not I want to watch a movie if I don't see the previews?"

"You can watch them on YouTube."

"Are you trying to be offensive?"

"No." He chuckles. "I'm offending you?"

"Yes."

"You got a problem with previews on YouTube?"

"I got a problem with you talking during the fucking previews." I narrow my eyes. "Why are you here? You never answered."

"To see a movie."

"A movie." I shake my head. "You didn't even know what movie I was watching until you got here. How'd you know I was even here?"

"It's one o'clock on a Sunday. Where else would you be?"

I sit back in my seat and look at the screen again. It's interesting to me that he doesn't even think me going home with Brian and still being at his place is a possibility and for some reason that pisses me off. He probably had Rebecca at the house and got rid of her this morning and then got bored and for some wild reason decided to come here. I swallow.

"I went home with Brian. I could've still been at his place," I say and hope he doesn't hear the massive lie in that statement.

"You stayed at the frat house?" Mav asks after a moment.

"Yep."

"Hm."

"How was your date?"

"It was great. We really hit it off and connected. We're going out again soon."

"Hm." I cross my arms.

"Why is it that every time I bring her up you act like you don't like her?"

"I don't know what you're talking about." I swallow, squeezing my arms just a little tighter across my chest before uncrossing them all together and setting a hand on the armrest between us.

Maverick doesn't say anything to that and I begin breathing a little easier as I watch the rest of the previews. Maybe he'll leave it alone. I probably shouldn't have told him that I stayed with Brian last night. It's not like he doesn't have ways of finding out, considering they play on the same damn team. Dammit, Rocky. That was dumb. Oh well. The movie starts and I completely relax and let the thoughts of Brian and Rebecca and Maverick drift away as I focus on the screen in front of us.

"You think we'll have the theatre all to ourselves?" Maverick whispers after a while. "That's wild."

"The fact that you're still trying to have a conversation with me is wild."

"Sorry." He picks up his bucket of popcorn and starts eating, then sets the bucket in front of me. "Want some?"

"No, thank you."

As the movie continues to play, we start laughing and Mav keeps his commentary to a minimum now that he's invested. I'm completely engrossed in the movie when Maverick sets his hand on mine. It's so sudden and unexpected that I jolt and sit upright.

"I . . ." He takes his hand away and sits upright as well, the movement setting us front to front, much closer than we were before. I search his eyes. He searches mine. My heart is pounding uncontrollably.

"You what?"

"I don't know. I just . . . I don't know," he says, his voice low.

He looks as nervous as I feel and he never looks nervous, which in turn makes me feel even more nervous. I swallow and lick my lips. His eyes drop to my mouth and he inches forward. There's nothing in this world, no movie, no popcorn, no person, that can make me look away now, and as I take the initiative and get closer to him and our breath dances between us, I don't know how I'll find it in me to pull away from this. I don't want to.

"Rocky." His voice is a rough whisper that scrapes through me, tearing me open. I shift so that I'm on my knees now, facing him, the armrest the only thing keeping me from pouncing on him right now.

"Just fucking kiss me already," I whisper, practically begging, because my mother taught me never to take initiative but damn it seems like such a dumb idea now.

His lips finally touch mine and if I thought my heart might beat out of my chest before, I was wrong, because it's beating so fast and hard, I can barely breathe. I open my mouth to welcome his tongue, shivering when I feel it, moaning when one of his large hands comes up and cups my face to take control of this kiss, his other hand exploring the side of my arm, bringing goosebumps all over my body. It deepens quickly, this mistaken kiss that feels so right in spite of itself. I hook my leg over the seat and Maverick pulls me so that I'm straddling him, my stomach flipping at the feel of him between my legs, large and hard, and too good not to rock against.

"Fuck. Rocky." He moans against me and breaks the kiss briefly, breathing heavily against me.

For a second, I think he may stop, but both hands grip my waist and he rocks against me, his mouth on the side of my neck, his tongue exploring. I grab a handful of his curls and continue moving against him as I lean forward and kiss his neck all the way up to the shell of his ear, licking it and tugging it into my mouth, eliciting another deep groan from him. He makes me feel wild and uninhibited, completely at odds with who I normally am, what I normally do. It's terrifying and electric. Completely all-consuming.

"You need to stop, Rock. I can't take it." His voice is

strained as he grips my hips so that I'm no longer grinding against his erection. We're both panting now.

"But I don't want to stop."

"And I don't want to fuck you in the back row of a movie theatre."

"Why not?" I frown, pulling back slightly. "If I was Rebecca or Tina, Carissa, or Mauve you would."

It's embarrassing that I know the names of most of the women he's fucked but it doesn't matter right now because right now it feels like he's turning me away after I was so ready to do more and . . . I shake my head, exhaling as I climb off his lap and go back to my seat.

"Rocky."

"No. I don't want to hear it. I'm going to finish watching the movie and go about my day and pretend that never happened."

"Rocky." He reaches for me.

"Stop." I yank my hand and shoot him a glare. "Maybe you should learn to take a hint. I'm staying at Leyla's for a reason. I come to the movies by myself for a reason."

"Okay." He pulls back, blinking slowly. After a moment, he grabs his popcorn and drink and stands up. "Enjoy your movie."

I don't watch him leave because my heart can't handle more destruction right now, but once I'm sure he's gone, I bury my face in my hands and start to cry.

"What'd you think?" Mom asks me when she calls me after the movie is over.

"It was whatever."

"That's what I said. Your father loved it, as expected."

"Hey, I didn't say I loved it, I said it was good," Dad says. "Hi, Rocky."

"Hey, Dad."

"What's wrong, babe?"

"Nothing," I say, even though I know I definitely sound like I'm pouting.

"Doesn't sound like nothing. Is it soccer?" Dad asks. "Is it your teammates?"

"What? No." I scoff. "My teammates are awesome."

"Is it a boy?" Mom asks, a knowing tone in her voice.

"I don't want to talk about it."

"What boy?" Dad asks loudly, his Jamaican accent suddenly clear and pronounced.

"I don't want to talk about it, Dad."

"Well, you better start telling me his name so I know whose ass I need to knock."

"Dad."

"Mike. Stop." That's Mom. "Sweetheart, you do you. If you wanna talk about this, call me later."

"Sure." I sigh. I've been parked outside of the theatre

for twenty minutes and I don't know what to do next. I can't go home and I don't want to keep hiding out at Leyla's, but I just might have to.

"Talk later then. If he hurts you, he's dead," Dad adds.

"Okay, Dad." I laugh. "I love you guys. Bye."

They say their goodbyes and I hang up the phone and head back to Leyla's.

Chapter Seventeen

"There's a party tonight and before you say no and tell me we already went to one last night, this is a mixer of sorts and Coach wants us to go."

"Coach? When did she say this?"

"She emailed a little while ago."

I look at Leyla. "Where is it and why? I feel like we've been to three of these mixers already."

"I have no idea what to wear to this mixer," Ashley says when she walks out of the room. "Do you know what we're supposed to wear?"

"Little black dresses?" Leyla asks. "That's what we wore last time."

"You wore a black suit and converse," I remind her.

"Right, because that's my version of a little black dress."

The Rulebreaker

"Do you have to go home to get yours?" Ash asks. "We can do our makeup at your place on our way there."

"Yeah, I guess that's a good idea."

When we step into the house, the new J Cole album is on at full-blast and Colson is walking around in nothing but his underwear, which, with the huge bulge, leaves very little to the imagination.

"Colson, what the hell? We have rules about this!" I shout.

"Yeah, Colson, what the hell?" Ashley raises an appreciative eyebrow and zones in on his dick.

"Ashley." I nudge her.

"What?" She laughs.

"Sorry, you're not my type, Ash." Colson chuckles.

"I'm not your type? Everyone is your type."

"None of Rocky's friends are my type. I like to fuck and leave and that's kind of impossible if you're always hanging around my roommate."

"Why are you parading around the house half-naked? We have rules about this," I say.

"Mav told me you were staying with your friends, so I figured it was safe. How was I supposed to know you were coming home?"

"Can you lower the music?" Leyla shouts.

"I would, but it's not my music. Mav is in his room with ... someone, and I guess he doesn't want us to hear what he's doing." Colson winks.

"Ew," Ashley says.

"Gross," Leyla adds.

"Unbelievable," I mutter as I stomp to my bedroom, knowing my friends will follow, but not caring at the moment.

The rage starts in my chest and blooms as I get my things ready for the party. By the time I shower, I'm more upset than I was when I started. The music is off though, which means he's done doing whatever he was doing. I think about the movie theatre just earlier today, about his lips on mine and his hands on my body, and I feel like vomiting when I envision him doing those things with someone else. I shouldn't have kissed him. I shouldn't have straddled him or let him touch me. I definitely shouldn't have because at least before all of this I wasn't sure about my feelings for him but now they're clear. I've completely fallen for my best friend and I feel like a complete idiot for it. It's not like I can escape him. I can't stay at Leyla and Ashley's forever. There's no room for me there. Looking for another place isn't an option. I don't have the time or money to do that right now. I berate myself for the kiss again, and again, until I decide that there's nothing I can do about it now except move forward and past it and leave it behind. Leyla and Ashley help me with my hair and makeup, Leyla straightens it, which I rarely do because it takes so much work to make my otherwise curly hair completely straight unless I go to a hair salon that's equipped to handle it and I don't have time or money for that either. Leyla's good at this though. She was blessed with similar curls and raised with four sisters.

"Damn," Ashley says, looking at me in the mirror. "You look fucking gorgeous, Rocky."

"Look at how long your hair is! You should let me do this more often," Leyla says, nodding her head slowly in appreciation. "You always look good but this is just . . . " She lets her words trail and does a chef's kiss.

"Thanks. I really do love it." I look at myself in the mirror and don't even see myself looking back at me.

I don't even bother with coyness, because dammit, I look amazing. My makeup is completely overdone with the smoky eyes and fake lashes, but it looks so good. I feel sexy in my little black dress that's tight and definitely way above my knees. My toned, muscular legs look extra defined in the sky-high heels I'm wearing, too—Jimmy Choo's I borrowed from Ash.

"I feel like we're going to need an after-party to go to," Leyla says, looking at the three of us. "We look way too good to waste it on people we see all the time."

"Agreed," I say.

"Totally," Ashley adds. "Reese—baseball Reese—is having a party at his place. The softball girls are going."

"Fuck yeah, sign me up for softball girls," Leyla says, smiling wide. "Are you down, Barnes? Or are you going to be a Party Pooper Rex?"

I think about Maverick again and hold my head high. "I'm absolutely down. I'm so down that I'm getting drunk tonight."

"Oooohhh," they both say, making the three of us fall into a fit of laughter.

"Has one drink, gets drunk, the end," Ashley adds.

"Fuck you. I can handle two drinks." I laugh.

"We shall see." Leyla takes a selfie of the three of us quickly and we walk out of my room.

"You took ten hours," Colson says. He's dressed in a black suit, black button-down, no tie, and black high converse. "But holy shit y'all look good."

"Thanks." I smile.

"Dude, your hair's long as hell." He walks over and touches it lightly. "So silky."

"Thanks. My work here is done," Leyla announces.

I hear a group of guys talking nearby and glance over to see Maverick, some of his teammates, and his brother Mitchell standing around the television where two of them are playing FIFA on the PlayStation. Maverick looks over, his eyes widening when he spots me. I feel my heart quicken as his eyes caress every inch of my body. When he meets my gaze again, I see the clear lust in his eyes as he licks his lips and says a quiet, "Damn."

"Let's go." Ashley pulls my hand and I tear my attention away from Maverick and back to my friends.

"You sure you don't want a shot before you go?" Colson's pouring tequila in a slew of glasses and small plastic cups.

"I'll take one." I walk forward.

"Uh-oh, she wasn't kidding about the drinking," Leyla says.

"I told you." I raise an eyebrow, take the glass from Colson, and the four of us take a shot together.

I shiver as the liquid runs through my veins and laugh when the three of them start poking at me about the drinking. I shoot one last glance in Maverick's direction and find that he's still staring at me, before I turn with my friends and leave. I should probably talk to him and apologize for earlier. I hate arguing with him and not clearing the air about things, but I'm also hurt right now, so I decide to sit with my feelings a little longer. At the end of the day, Maverick and I will always be in each other's lives one way or another, but these emotions I feel for him are too strong to deny and too terrifying to name. I need to know what I'm going to say the next time I'm able to talk to him seriously so that I don't hurt either one of us.

Chapter Eighteen

Maverick

"Why'd they leave?" Mitchell asks as we watch Rocky and her friends leave. "Aren't they going to the same place we are?"

"I guess they don't want to ride with us."

"Weird." My brother looks over at me. "Is Rocky still pissed off at you because of the party you had here without telling her?"

"No."

"Something else?"

"No. I don't know. Why are you asking so many questions?" I shoot him a look.

"Calm down, I'm just being a good brother. Jagger isn't here to ask his thousand and one questions, so it's my responsibility to make sure everything is okay."

"Everything is fine."

"You sure?" He assesses me closely. "You've been acting weird as hell lately."

"Everything is fine, Mitch. I'm just focused on hockey and school."

"Really? Cause Mom told me something about Rocky and—"

"She what?" I blink. "Do you have nothing better to do than to discuss my private life?"

"Private life?" He laughs, throwing his head back. "Oh, sorry, I didn't realize you had a fucking private life. What are you, an A-list celebrity? I'm your brother, you asshole. Why didn't you tell me about Rocky?"

"There's nothing to tell."

"That's not what Mom said." He raises an eyebrow.

"You are such an old lady. Why are you gossiping with Mom?"

"Oh, yeah." He scoffs. "You gossip with Mom all the freaking time. It's how I know about this, to begin with."

"Well, according to Mom, you're lusting after Misty and haven't done anything about it."

"Mom said that?" His jaw drops. "She said lusting?"

"She didn't say lusting, but it was clear enough that's what she meant."

"Well, I'm not." He frowns. "Why are you discussing that anyway?"

"See? It's not cool. Stop talking about me behind my back."

"You act like we're talking bad about you. We discussed you in passing."

"In passing." I roll my eyes. "What does that even mean?"

"It means stop being so damn weird about it and talk to me."

"I'm not being weird." I squeeze my eyes shut. When I open them, my brother's green eyes are still on mine. "I don't even know what's going on, okay? We kissed this morning and then she acted like it was the end of the world and basically told me to fuck off and that she didn't want to be with me."

"What?" Mitch looks as confused as I feel. "Rocky said that?"

"Yes."

"Hm." He shakes his head. "No wonder you're acting strange."

"I just need to speak to her and pray things go back to normal."

"Is that what you want?" Mitch searches my face.

"Yo, let's go," Colson shouts from somewhere in the house. "Ubers are here."

"I just want my friend back," I say as my brother and I walk toward the door.

"Even if that means you'll have to pretend you're not falling for her?"

"Yep."

"That's wild, Maverick." Mitchell shakes his head.

"Life's wild." I shrug a shoulder. "I'm just trying to live mine in peace."

Peace is bullshit. I'm watching Brian and Rocky from the far side of the room and I'm hating every excruciating minute of it. He keeps touching her. She keeps laughing. They keep drinking. I keep thinking about this afternoon, how I had her in my lap, how perfect she felt against me, how easy it would have been for me to fuck her right there. I don't regret stopping it from happening, but I definitely regret how I reacted to everything afterwards. I should've stayed. I should've demanded a conversation. I should've explained myself and why I didn't fuck her when she gave the okay. I should've told her a million things, but I didn't because even though I know I give the best advice out of my friend group, I can't seem to take my own.

"You're really just going to keep staring at her?" Mitchell asks, standing beside me.

"I don't understand why they serve drinks at these events."

"Says the guy drinking a beer." He chuckles.

"Yeah, well, according to my count, Rocky has had at least five shots. She doesn't even drink normally, so you know this won't end well."

"And you're going to babysit her all night like it's your job," Mitch says, shaking his head. "Maybe she wants to be with Brian. Maybe she wants to let loose and go home with him."

I shoot him a glare. "I dare him to try."

"Are y'all going to the after-party with us?" Ashley asks, walking over to us.

"What after-party?" I ask.

"Oh, Rocky didn't tell you?" Ashley frowns before her face shifts into an "oh shit was I not supposed to say anything" expression that makes my already heated blood start to simmer.

"Is it Reese's party?" Mitchell asks.

"Yeah." Ashley smiles. "So, you did know about it. I mean, duh, of course you did."

"I guess we'll see you there," I say. I wait for her to walk away before turning to my brother. "I guess we know where Brian and Rocky are going next."

"So, what's the play here? We're going to follow them around all night?"

"You have anything better to do?" I look around for show.

"No, asshole." He rolls his eyes. "But just so you know, I did talk Misty into going on a date with me."

"Oh wow. A date."

Mitch chuckles, shaking his head. "I would say you need to get laid, but from what I heard you got laid today."

"Today?" I stop walking and glance over at him. "What the hell are you talking about?"

"When I got to your place Colson said you were in your room playing the new J Cole CD with someone."

"Okay?" My frown deepens.

"You only do that when you want to block out the noise."

"What?" I laugh, and once I start, I can't stop because of the ridiculousness of this conversation. "First of all, my door was open and I had Ray and Erwin in there with me listening to the album, so unless you guys are accusing me of having a gay threesome, nothing happened. Colson said this?"

"Yes." He raises his eyebrows.

"Colson's an idiot then."

"I mean, you said it, not me."

Reese lives in an apartment in the same building as my brother. Same floor, too. It's two to three guys per apartment and they seem to share everything and never get sick of each other. Even though I live with Colson and we play together, this feels like too much. It's like taking the locker room home or something. Some of my coaches actually call the baseball players "the locker room bros" as a joke. I'm standing on the balcony with my brother and a few of our friends, but I'm not really contributing much to the conversation tonight because I'm too hyper-focused on what Rocky is doing. She's still hanging with Brian. They're still touching and talking and laughing and I don't know how much longer I can just stand here without intervening. I swing my attention back to Mitch, who's talking about some assignment Misty is doing and how she's interviewing everyone, when the door opens and Rocky appears.

"Mitch," she whispers. "I need your key."

"For what?" Mitch frowns.

"I have to pee and I don't wanna use the bathroom here because it's gross." She looks at the rest of us before looking at Reese. "No offense, Reese."

"None taken." He chuckles. "It was probably someone at the party though because I keep my shit clean. No pun intended." He cringes.

"I'll take you." Mitch walks over.

"No, I'll take her." I step aside and block him slightly.

"Okay." My brother hands me his keys and shoots me a warning as if to say *don't fuck this up*. I grab the keys and turn to Rocky, who starts walking beside me.

My brother is two doors down. When I open the door to his apartment, it smells like it was just cleaned, and I know that's the case since Ms. Ana just went to our house yesterday and she cleans ours back-to-back. Rocky rushes inside and goes straight to the guest bathroom. I walk around, hands in my pockets, as I wait. The view of the city is nice from this building. I turn around when I hear Rocky's heels against the wood floors behind me.

"It's such a nice night," she says, walking over and I can't control the way my heart pounds against my chest with each step she takes.

"It is." I turn back to the windows briefly, then look at her again. "I've been hoping to talk to you all day."

She side-eyes me. "Okay."

I'm thankful my hands are still in my pockets because I'm dying to touch her. For ten years I've been nothing more than her friend and now suddenly I want, need, more. It's insanity, yet here I am, a lunatic falling for my friend.

"I guess I should apologize for flipping out on you earlier," she says.

"I'm sorry I kissed you." I lick my lips and keep my eyes straight ahead so she can't see the lie in my eyes.

"It's okay. Truly. I overreacted."

"You didn't." I turn to her. "If you didn't want me to kiss you, or touch you, you should have reacted that way. There's no other way to react."

"I didn't say that." She bites her lip and looks away.

"How's this thing with Brian going?"

"It's going." She smiles. I love to see her smile, but I hate that he's the reason for it. "How's the thing with Rebecca?"

"Could be better." I shrug a shoulder. Could be better if it was her I liked, I should say, but don't. "You still haven't given me more rules to follow. You know, to woo her off her feet."

"Ah, well, flowers," she says, checking one off the list. "Words. Women like words. But you have to mean them. You can't go around saying things you don't mean." She shoots me a look. "What else . . . touch, women like to be touched, but not overboard like grabbing her ass in public without having that level of comfort, you know? Just hand-holding kind of things. Breakfast. Or any meal, really. Food is always good. Loyalty." She searches my eyes. "It's important that you're not fucking around behind our backs. Listen to her when she speaks, even if she's talking about things that bore you. And finally, make her feel like she's important."

"That's it?"

"That's it." She smiles with a shrug.

"Okay."

"Okay." She turns and starts walking toward the door.

"So, you're going home with Brian again?"

"Huh?" She glances at me over her shoulder.

"You said you went home with Brian last night and

things are looking like they're going well between you two, so I guess I assumed . . ."

"Oh. Nah. I need to sleep in my bed tonight."

"I don't know when you want to leave, but I'm getting ready to head out," I say, hoping against all odds that she'll leave as well.

"I'll come with."

And suddenly, all is right in the world again.

Chapter Nineteen

Rocky

Evidentially, tequila makes my head spin and does not make me sleepy, but somehow, I feel like I'm finally falling asleep, when I hear my bedroom door open and shut and feel the bed dip beside me.

"Rocky," Maverick whispers.

"Hm?"

"You looked beautiful tonight."

"What?" I blink in the dark and turn to face him. "What are you talking about?"

"You looked beautiful tonight."

"Okay. Thanks. Why didn't you say this earlier?" I yawn.

"Because I'm an idiot."

"Agreed." I laugh, propping my face on my hand. My blinds are open, so my room has an orange glow from the streetlight and I can sort of see Mav. "I take it you couldn't sleep?"

"No." He sighs heavily and mimics my pose.

"What's up?"

"Do you really regret the kiss?"

My heart bumps my chest a little harder. "What?"

"The kiss. Do you really regret it that much?"

"No, but you obviously did."

"Why would you say that?"

"Because you apologized last time and when I got here, you were in your room with someone, playing that J Cole album."

"Jesus Christ," he mutters, falling onto his back. He looks up at me. "Are you serious right now?"

"Yeah."

"I was with Erwin and Ray. Colson's a fucking moron. That's how rumors start."

"Oh."

"You thought I was with a girl?" He sits up rapidly. I do the same.

"Yeah."

"After I kissed you like that? After I touched you? After you were all over me? You thought I'd go and sleep with someone else?"

"Yeah." I shrug. "Why wouldn't you?"

"Rocky." He shakes his head. "You're my best friend. Before anything else, you're my best friend."

"I know," I whisper, licking my lips and nodding. "Is that why you wouldn't go further?"

"I . . . " He exhales heavily, glancing away momentarily. "Yes and no."

"Yes and no? This should be good." I cross my arms.

"I don't mean it in a bad way." He brings a hand up, his thumb caressing the side of my face. "I just don't want to do anything to hurt you."

"But what if I don't care, Maverick? What if I want to put myself in a position to get hurt? It's my choice."

"As your best friend, I would never let you do that."

I close my eyes and relish the feel of his calloused fingers on my face. He's never touched my face like this before. Not really anyway. Maybe once, back when we were sixteen and I fractured my ankle and he was trying to calm me down while the paramedics arrived at the soccer park. Still, it feels different this time. Probably because of that damn kiss that he regrets so much.

"Rocky." The way he says my name, uneven and uncertain, makes me open my eyes and look into his again. "That kiss? It was magical, but if we go any further, it would change everything."

"It doesn't have to change anything."

"You know it will."

"It might not." I bring a hand up and cusp it around his wrist. "If I were any other girl, you would have kept going."

"But you're not any other girl. You're you."

"I'm starting to think that's not such a good thing right now." I glance away briefly. "You know how you hear about people who practice kissing with their best friends because they know that things won't go too far?"

Mav raises an eyebrow. "Yeah."

"So, I was thinking we could do something like that."

"You want to be my booty call?"

"Maybe."

He chuckles. "You can't be my booty call, Rocky."

"Why not?" I frown. "I'm serious. You have other booty calls."

"Yeah, because I don't care about them. It's a mean thing to say, but I don't. I didn't even do that until recently. You know that."

"Because you were still hung up on your ex," I say.

"I was not hung up on my ex." He chuckles. "Do you realize how ridiculous this entire conversation is?"

"I do." I press my lips together. Maverick searches my face. "I want you."

"Why now?"

"I don't know. Why'd you kiss me? Why'd you hold my hand? Why now?"

"I don't know." He folds his hands on his lap and looks at me. "Okay, I do know. I've liked you forever, Rocky. You've always been the prettiest, smartest, funniest girl in my book, but I love that I get to keep you forever, you know? I don't know if I can keep a girlfriend forever, but you, my best friend? Definitely."

"So, hook up with me and pretend it never happened."

He laughs. "You're serious about that."

"I am. I never wanted to lose my virginity before, because of well, you know."

"Because you've been waiting for someone worth giving it to," he says, reciting back my exact reason.

"Exactly."

"And you think you've found that in me somehow? The guy who swore he'd never become a manwhore, yet somehow did."

"You're not a manwhore, Mav." I roll my eyes. "Sure, you've hooked up with more girls this year than ever, but you're just doing normal college stuff."

"I don't deserve you."

"I don't care. I'm not asking you whether or not you deserve me. I want to do this with you and get it over with so that at least I know the first man I slept with was someone I trust and love."

"Why not wait for someone you trust and love for real?"

"This is for real."

"You know what I mean."

"Because. I've waited and nothing has happened."

"What about Brian?"

"What about him?" I frown.

"You stayed at his place the other day."

"I lied." I bite my lip and glance away. "I was at Leyla's."

"Why would you lie about that?"

"Because I didn't want to sound like a loser."

"Wow. You think not sleeping with someone will make you sound like a loser? Who are you and what have you done with my friend?"

"Mav." I groan. "Are we doing this or what?"

I watch as he thinks about it. I can practically hear his thoughts, everything he's trying to weigh out in his head. If we do this, our friendship will change. We both know that. If we don't, I'll lose my virginity to some frat boy and it won't be memorable. He knows that too. It'll boil down to which one he'd rather live with and I'm really hoping the answer to that is as simple for him as it is for me. I'd rather do this with him than anyone else because even if our friendship changes, it won't be broken. We've been through too much together for that to ever happen. He brings a hand back up to my face, beckoning my eyes to his, and I know before he says anything that his mind has been made up.

A flutter of butterflies swarms my belly as he leans in and kisses me, his lips touching mine ever so gently. I sit up on my knees and hold both sides of his face, deepening the kiss. It's soft and sweet, unlike everything Mav makes himself out to be, this massive hockey player with a chip on his shoulder who people are afraid of on the ice, but is really the kindest, sexiest human being. His hands make their way down my arms as he starts to undress me slowly, taking my shirt off and tossing it. He rocks back slightly on his knees and looks at me.

"Damn," he breathes out, closing his eyes for a moment before opening them again as he attacks, his hands and mouth on my breasts, playing with my sensitive nipples. "Damn, damn, damn," he says between licks and sucks.

"I think I'm going to come," I whisper, "if you keep doing this."

I'm not joking. If the pool between my legs is any indication, I really think I might. I've pleasured myself before, with my hands, a small vibrator I bought a couple of years ago, closing my legs tightly until I find release, but in all that time I don't think I have ever been this wet, this needy, this horny. He moves his mouth from my breasts and makes his way down my body. I reach out to touch him and gasp when I close my hand around him. He's so hard and so large, I'm almost positive he'll rip me apart. It's a price I'm willing to pay. We kiss again, wantonly. Our mouths in a frenzy, our hands bewildered, touching, probing, our breaths ragged. He runs his thumbs over my nipples as I undress him, pinches them as I take off my panties. Pulls back again to examine me and shakes his head with a low, deep chuckle, that I can only categorize as turned on, which is perfect since I am so turned on, and seeing him naked for the first time is mind-blowing. He's perfection. I already knew that, but now that he doesn't have anything on his skin at all, it's confirmed. Perfection. He reaches for me again, his mouth soft on my lips, my neck.

"I really want you," I breathe, because I don't know what else to say to convey this need.

"You have no idea how much I want you." He keeps kissing me, exploring my body with his mouth.

He makes me lie back and makes his way down to the mound between my legs, his tongue flicking, groaning against me with each taste. My legs begin to shake. I grab a handful of his curls to pull him away, keep him there, I don't know, it's all too much. I've never felt this way before. I come again. It's both surprising and delicious. As he moves over me, he wipes his mouth and my heart feels like it might just pop out of my chest.

"I'm clean," I say quickly. "And you know I'm on the pill because—"

"I know," he finishes. "And you know I've never—"

"I know," I finish. "And if you don't feel comfortable sleeping with me without one I totally—"

He silences me with a kiss, one drenched in my desire. I moan into his mouth and moan again when he flicks my nipple with his thumb and forefinger. Fuck. He's going to kill me. I've always heard friends say they never forget their first, but I didn't understand why until this moment. I know without a doubt I'll never forget this. Ever. It's terrifying. And when he begins thrusting inside me slowly, shallow enough that I don't feel like I'm going to break open, but deep enough that I just might, it's electrifying. He goes slow, slow, with such care, searching my face for any sort of discomfort, and all I want to do is cry openly. It hurts. A lot. But then, it feels so good. He feels so good. Once he sees that I'm okay, that I'm not in pain, and I'm nodding to convey it to him, he pulls back ever so slightly, and lifts my hips up. His hands grip my rib cage as he begins to fuck me a little harder. He takes one hand away from my torso and brings it between my legs, making my eyes roll to the back of my head. I begin to shake.

"It's too much," I argue.

"Shh."

"Mav." My eyes pop open and look at him. He's biting his lower lip like he's barely holding on, his arms flexing each muscle as he pounds into me, and if I thought he'd ever been sexier, I was wrong.

"Let go, baby. You have to just let go," he says, low, husky, barely keeping control.

And I do.

I let go.

The orgasm washes over me so quickly and so hard, that I scream. I feel his cum inside of me, hot and sticky. He stays inside me for a moment once we're both breathing.

"Was it . . . was I okay?" I ask.

"Were you okay?" He raises an eyebrow, letting out a ragged breath. "You're fucking perfect, Rocky. Perfect."

The way he looks at me, the way he says it, with such reverence, I know he's not lying. Then again, Maverick would never lie to me.

Chapter Twenty

Maverick

"CRUZ, GET YOUR HEAD OUTTA YOUR ASS AND SCORE A fucking goal out there," Coach yells. "You've been off your game all fucking day."

I nod, huffing out a frustrated breath. Sex is supposed to make you relax, not infiltrate and cloud every single one of your thoughts, but here I am, playing like an asshole because I can't seem to stop thinking about Rocky naked and straddling me, naked and lying beneath me, calling out my name when she comes. Fuck. I take a deep breath and focus on the game. I've never gotten hard while wearing a cup and my gear on the ice, but there's a first time for everything and I definitely don't need that in my life right now. The puck clicks against my stick as I deke to the left, losing my opponent. I position myself so that I have a clear shot of the goal and wait. I always wait. It's something that drives both my teammates and coaches crazy. They think I should shoot it while I can and not risk someone coming and taking it from me, but I like taking my time. I like watching the goalie squirm, and the Ellis University new goalie, Nolan Astor, is my favorite opponent to go against. He doesn't squirm. Not even close. Nolan keeps his composure in every situation and that's what I love about this. I hit the puck and watch as he glides to the other side of the net and just as I think it's about to go in, he blocks it.

"Fuck," I scream.

"That's right, baby. Get that shit out of here," Nolan says behind me as I move to the other side of the rink.

I don't bother with a reaction because the best reaction would be to score a freaking goal on his ass. My team keeps moving.

"Yo, get your head in the damn game." Colson gets beside me.

"I know. I know."

"Do you though? They have two points on the board. We have zero. And you know those Ellis fuckers won't let us live this down."

"I know." I huff out a breath, adjust my mouthpiece, and push harder.

We block them from scoring on our side and when I take the puck again and skate down the rink, I do something Nolan doesn't expect from me—I don't stop. I just drive and score one in.

"Take that, fucker," I shout as I skate away. Nolan chuckles, shaking his head.

"Hey, Mav," Nolan shouts. I turn and skate backward. "Does your back hurt from carrying your whole team?"

I shake my head, but can't help laughing. I love my team, but sometimes it definitely feels that way.

After the game, which we lose by one point, we skate by the other team to shake their hands. I stop in front of Nolan and we hug quickly.

"How's everything up there?" I ask.

"Better than here." He raises a hand and runs it through his straight, dirty blond, shoulder-length hair.

"We're chillin' down here. What are you talking about?"

"You're chillin' for now. Your sports programs are about to go through some crazy shit."

"What are you talking about?"

"You seriously haven't heard?"

"Heard what?"

"They're looking into a drug ring going on here."

"Here, here?"

"Yeah."

"How do you know about it and I don't?"

"I stay informed, Cruz, that's why. I was going to text you about it, but I wasn't sure if you were involved."

"In a fucking drug ring?" I whisper-shout. "Why the hell would I be involved in that?"

"People do stupid shit for money and power." Nolan chuckles. "Then again, you definitely don't need any more money or power."

"No shit." I let out a laugh. I work hard to do well in school and on the ice, but because I'm fortunate enough to have the parents I have, I've never wanted for anything. "Do you have names of people involved?"

"Nope. I know it's a lot of football players and some baseball."

"Baseball?" I nearly shout as we skate off the ice.

"Your brother plays, right?"

"Yeah, but he's not involved in no drug ring. He doesn't need the money either."

"Dude, I don't know what's going on. I just know it's going to explode in everyone's face, and this ring goes all the way up to Ellis."

"Are you involved?" I raise an eyebrow.

"No, bro, of course not. Not directly anyway." He sighs heavily. "Let's just say, I'm keeping my head low for the time being."

"Meaning you are involved."

"I'm not."

"Your not-so-secret society is involved then."

Nolan shrugs.

"Fuck. I'm sorry, man." I give him a pat on the shoulder and another sideways hug. "If you need anything, you know I'm here."

"Thanks, man. I hope I won't need anything, but I'll let you know if I do."

When I get home, I head straight to the laundry room and shove everything in the washing machine before I head to Rocky's room. She had a game today as well so we always check up on each other to see how they went. As I walk there, my heart is pounding in my chest. I don't know why I'm nervous, considering I'm never nervous to see her. I open her door and find her room empty.

"Rocky?"

"In the bathroom."

"Oh." I walk into the room and plop down on the bed, but then I hear the whooshing of water. "You're in the tub?"

"Ice bath."

I stand up and walk over to the bathroom, unsure of whether or not I should walk inside. Normally, I would not, but I've already seen her naked. I leave my hand on the door for a moment and wait.

"Can I come in?" I ask finally.

"Um . . . yeah, I guess. I mean, nothing you haven't seen before, right?" She laughs awkwardly as I push the door open.

She's not wrong, but still, seeing her figure in that tub makes me stop breathing for a moment. I walk back outside, grab the chair she has by the desk in the room, and bring it inside, placing it beside the tub. I'm looking at her face since looking anywhere else would be dangerous right now.

"I see you've emptied out our freezer again." I smile as I look at all of the ice covering her. "How was your game?"

"We won. I scored both goals."

"Damn." I smile wide.

"How was yours?"

"We lost by one point."

"Ah, sorry." She pulls a face and sets a foot over the tub.

"Not your fault." I reach for her foot and start massaging it. "Ellis played like shit. We should have won, but I was distracted."

"You can't carry your entire team, Mav."

I laugh. "That's what their goalie said."

"Well, he's not wrong."

"I know, but you know how it is." I raise an eyebrow and keep massaging. She closes her eyes with a moan that goes straight to my nether regions. "Besides, you scored two goals today."

"I just happened to be at the right place at the right time." She smiles, eyes still closed, and I let my eyes drift down, to the clear water and the smooth caramel flesh beneath it that seems to awaken every cell in my being.

The ice moves and I get a glimpse of her perky brown nipples. It takes everything in me not to react. Not to get in the tub we definitely don't fit into together. I continue massaging her foot, then make my way up her calves, and when she moans again, I can't take it anymore. I stand up. Her eyes pop open and whatever she sees in my eyes is enough to get the point across. She sits up in the tub, and I lift her out of it as water swishes in every direction. Last time, I took my time with her. This time, I don't think I can. I'd never fucked anyone without a condom. Chalk it up to my parents and older brothers' continuous speeches about safety, but I've known Rocky my entire life. Outside of my immediate family, if I had to put my entire being in someone else's hands, it would be hers. I pull down my pants just to my knees, sit back on the chair, and position her between my legs as I kiss her, my tongue wild on hers, her hands gripping my hair tightly as she welcomes my cock into her pussy. Fuck. I've never felt anything like this before, and part of me doesn't know if I ever will.

I've been with enough women to know that this is special. This kind of unfiltered, wild, emotional sex is not the usual. The fact that it's happening with the ultimate girl of my dreams isn't a surprise, but it also absolutely sucks to be deep inside your best friend's pussy and know that you can't have it forever. For now, I let her ride me like I'm her personal cowboy. Like it's the last ride of her fucking life, and that's exactly what she does until we both come.

Chapter Twenty-One

Rocky

"BUT YOU'RE NOT DATING," LEYLA ASKS ACROSS FROM ME. "Just fucking?"

"It's complicated." I exhale. "We're not dating though, no."

"So, you're friends with benefits."

"I guess."

"And you can date other guys."

"I mean, I'm not dating another guy, which is why I'm in this situation, but I guess if I wanted to date another guy I could, yeah."

"Hm."

"What?" I cross my arms and wait for her to finish her veggie burger.

"I just think it's a dangerous game. If you do feel like

dating someone else, would he get in the way of that? Would you even tell him?"

"I mean, I always tell him."

"But that was before you started messing around."

"I don't think it's as big a deal as you're making it."

"Isn't it though? Wasn't he dating that girl Rebecca? What happened with all that?"

"I don't know. As far as I know, they only went on that one date."

"Messy," Leyla says. "This shit is messy."

"I know." I bite my lip. "His parents are coming down next weekend and want to take a little road trip to Charlotte to watch Jagger play. He scored one of those private lounges for them and they invited me to go along."

"Damn, that sounds fun!"

"It does, right?" I bite my lip. It sounds like so much fun, but now that I'm in this weird situation with Mav I'm not so sure.

"Where will you stay?"

"Jagger's mansion." I let out a laugh. "He and Jo bought like a ten-bedroom mansion."

"Ballers."

"I know." I smile.

I've known them just as long as I've known Maverick. Jagger, obviously, since they're brothers, but Josephine and her sister Misty I've known because their parents are friends with Mav's and in turn, mine. Dr. Canó even did my surgery when I hurt my foot, and then my knee, and I've seen him here a few times for stretching purposes.

"Anyway, it'll be fine," I say.

"If you say so, homegirl. This is your mess." Leyla crumples the wrapper her burger came in and stands up. "You ready for class?"

"Yep."

We walk in five minutes late and Maverick is the first person I spot. He's always the first person I spot, but even that feels different now. My heart tumbles into my stomach when his eyes find mine. Beside him, Rebecca is showing him something on her cell phone, and I feel myself go hot all over. It's not like I'm naïve enough to think he's given up on the Rebecca dream. Since we got here he's been saying that's his dream girl. Funny how she looks and acts the complete opposite of me. I don't let that thought marinate too long. I focus on finding a seat and then on the lecture. African Studies was a subject I picked because I thought it looked easy and I needed an elective, but it's become my favorite class to attend, probably because Ms. Malone makes it easy for us to get lost and invested in the history.

"So, he is still doing the Rebecca thing," Leyla whispers beside me.

I shoot her a look. "Don't start."

"I'm just saying, you can continue your thing with Brian if you wanted."

"There is no thing with Brian."

"Right. He's a bore. What about Jordan? The one who asked you out last semester. He was cute."

"Eh." I shrug. "No chemistry."

"What about Landon? The one we used to see at like every party. He's in your psych class, right?"

"I know who Landon is, Layla." I laugh, "yeah, he is in psych."

Landon is really cute, but I never really took him up on the offer to take me out because I was too distracted by my feelings for Maverick. I look at Maverick again and see Rebecca leaning into the side of his seat and whisper something in his ear. Whatever it is, makes her blush. I wait, and wait, but Maverick doesn't seem to react to it and Rebecca moves back to her seat. My heart leaps.

What does this mean?

Then, I berate myself. I was the one who told him things wouldn't change, that they didn't have to, and I'm sitting here dissecting body language. Maybe Leyla's right. Still, instead of setting up a legitimate date with Landon, I agree to a study date. We have a big psychology exam coming up and we both need to study for it anyway, so why not make it fun?

Chapter Twenty-Two

I'M SITTING IN TONY'S DRINKING WATER, WAITING FOR LANDON, when Maverick walks in. My body instantly reacts—pulse racing, heart flipping into the pit of my stomach. Mitchell walks in closely behind him, followed by Colson, and some other guys. They look like trouble and Maverick looks extra sexy. Mitch, Mav, and Colson are all wearing backward baseball caps, as if they were in a ninety's bad boy band or something alongside Marky Mark. My mom freaking loves Marky Mark. Well, back then, she did. In all her old photos, she has him plastered on the walls of the house where she grew up in Jamaica, which means his sex appeal was global, and I can see why, but he has nothing on these guys.

Colson spots me first, and nods one of those cool guy nods before heading to the table they normally sit at on Thursdays. Mitch looks over right after and nods and throws up a peace sign as he follows Colson. The rest of the guys look in my direction and do a little wave before Maverick finally sees me. When our eyes meet, I swear it's like everyone in this restaurant instantly disappears and that's just not good. He walks over to me and that's when I see he has a bouquet of white hydrangeas. I frown as I look back up. Is he meeting a girl here? *Rebecca*. I feel the color drain from my face as he reaches me.

"What's up?"

"What's wrong with you?" He slides into the booth, across from me.

"Nothing is wrong."

He sets the flowers on the table. I love them. I hate them. "You're waiting for Landon, aren't you?"

"Jesus," I grumble. "Do you find out about everything?"

"I saw him earlier. He was bragging." Mav's mouth tilts into a half-smile as he checks me out. "I can't blame him."

"What are you doing?"

"Talking to my bestie. Why?"

"Your bestie." That makes me laugh. I nod at the flowers between us. "Are you meeting Rebecca here?"

"Nope."

"Oh. Wow. You move on fast."

"You can say that." He looks like he's trying not to

laugh. Normally I'm in on the joke, so this is wild, this feeling of the unknown between us.

"You're so weird." I bite my lip and glance toward the door. Landon sees me and waves with a smile on his face. I sit up straighter. "Landon's here."

"I guess I'll let you be." Maverick slides out of the booth and walks over to my side, kissing me on the cheek. I ignore the way my body awakens with it.

"Don't forget your flowers," I say, making him chuckle against my face, which in turn makes me go hot all over.

"The flowers are for you, bestie," he whispers in my ear before pulling back and walking away.

I know without a shadow of a doubt that I'm blushing fiercely and it doesn't matter that I'm brown, or that I'm wearing makeup, or that I'm trying my best to stay calm. Freaking Maverick. I take the flowers and place them beside me, smiling up at Landon when he finally reaches me.

"It's not your birthday, is it?" He looks at the flowers with a frown.

"Oh. No." I laugh. "Inside joke."

"You must have a lot of those." He shakes his head as he sits across from me, setting his backpack beside him. "Being that you've known each other since you were tweens and all."

"Yeah. Tons of inside jokes." I keep smiling, hoping my blush will go away soon. I take another sip of water and set it down.

"He warned me about you earlier."

"What?" My smile drops. "What about me?"

"Nothing bad, just not to break your heart or something. I mean, he didn't say that exactly, but he basically said if I hurt you he'd kill me and feed me my balls or something. He seemed upset about the whole thing," Landon says casually. "But then Colson told me you've been friends forever and I realized it's probably something he says to all the guys you hang out with just in case. I mean, I do that with my little sisters."

"Hm. Nice to know." I reach into my backpack and pull out my psych book. Landon does the same. "How many sisters do you have?"

"Two. Might as well be twenty, as troublesome as they are." He flashes me a smile. He's really freaking handsome and has perfect white teeth that stand out against his dark skin.

"Well, they're lucky to have you." I smile. "I'm an only child and I always wanted an older brother."

"From the looks of it, you lucked out and got three. Those Cruz brothers are definitely loyal."

"Ha. Yeah, they are." I open the book and start leafing through it. Anything to get out of a conversation where Maverick and I are anything like siblings.

I can barely remember the last time I looked at him like a brother. Thankfully, Landon takes the hint and moves the conversation to the impending test we have. We study for a while. Long enough that the server comes by at least six times to refill my water and ask if we want more bread or any more food because they're about to shut down the kitchen and the DJ is about to start playing.

"You wanna stay here or go someplace else?" Landon asks.

"Are we going to keep studying or just chill?"

He looks around, waves at a few guys he knows, and looks back at me. "I mean, I love Tony's on a Thursday, but if you'd rather hit up Franklin Street or a brewery or something, I'm down too."

"We can stay here." I smile and start getting out of the booth. "I need to take this to my car and go to the restroom."

"I'm going to get a drink at the bar then since we're not going to stay at this table. I'll be in that general area." He signals toward his friends.

I nod, grab my things, and head outside. The chilly wind hits me as soon as I step out there and suddenly I'm grateful I pulled a jean jacket out of my closet at the last minute. You never know what the weather will be from one moment to the next in North Carolina. That's one thing I learned quickly after moving here. I lock my car and walk back inside, beelining to the bathrooms. Once I'm done and finish washing my hands, I check myself in the mirror. I still look fine. My curls are extra voluminous tonight after the deep conditioning I did this morning and my makeup is still on point. I'm feeling myself as I walk out of the bathroom and find Maverick standing there, holding a drink in his hand.

"Fancy meeting you here." I smile at him.

"How'd your study date go?"

"Well, that portion of the date is over."

"And there's another portion coming up now?" He takes a sip of his drink. I step forward and take the glass out of his hand, smelling it before taking a small sip.

"It's good. Tequila?"

"And club soda."

"I don't normally like club soda, but this is good."

"You love lime, so it's probably that."

"True." I smile. "Anyway, yeah, we're just going to hang out here for a while. What are you up to tonight?"

"Playing masochistic games. You know, the usual."

I frown. "What?"

"Nothing." He chuckles, taking another sip and glancing away. "I'm going to hang out here as well." He looks at me. "Are you going to the Halloween party Saturday night?"

"I have a game that afternoon. I guess it depends on how badly I get beat up."

"I'm always available for massages." He winks.

"Mav." My heart pounds harder in my chest.

"What?" He cocks his head to the side, shooting me

that flirty smile that I know for a fact makes women crazy, and right now, I'm women.

"Why'd you bring me flowers?" I cross my arms and rock slightly.

He smiles, standing upright. "Why do you think I brought you flowers?"

"I don't know, that's why I'm asking."

"It's on your list."

I blink. "My list?"

"The list of things to do in order to impress someone. You said to give her flowers."

"But . . . you gave them to me." My heart is racing now.

"Did I impress you?"

"No."

"No?" He raises an eyebrow. "Wrong kind of flower?"

"No, the flowers are beautiful, I just, I don't understand why you would want to impress me, to begin with."

"That's a good question." Mav chuckles, glancing away momentarily. "I think Landon's waiting for you. Go have fun. We'll talk later."

"Okay." I feel my frown deepen, but we both head toward the main area, where everyone is hanging out.

To say I'm confused is an understatement. He brought me flowers and flirts with me but then backs off and tells me to go have fun with some other guy? It's not like Maverick. Once he gets his eyes on a girl he usually goes all in and he's definitely not the sharing type, so the fact that he's willing to share me is all wrong. Then again, maybe I'm the one who's crazy for thinking he'd want more with me. Mom always says when someone shows you who they are, you should believe them, but I know him. I've seen all of the faces of Maverick Cruz and so far, there hasn't been one I haven't liked. Unfortunately for both of us, even though I swore up and down that I would not let sex between us change our relationship, it obviously has, but if he wants to play this game and act like he's okay seeing me with another man, who am I to not take advantage of that freedom? On that note, I turn to Landon and start talking to him.

Chapter Twenty-Three

Maverick

"YOU LOOK LIKE YOU'RE ABOUT READY TO KILL SOMEONE. Who we fightin'?" That's Colson, and he's not kidding, he's ready to fight. I've seen that look on his face one too many times.

"I'm good." I take another sip of my drink.

"And you're drinking tequila. You're going to box people up tonight," he shouts excitedly.

"You're wild." I chuckle.

I don't normally drink and when I do it's definitely not tequila, but I saw a TikTok the other day that made me want to try this, and I actually really like it. The lights to Tony's dim and more and more people spill in. It's definitely the place to be on a Thursday. You wouldn't know it if you come here for lunch or dinner, but once they clear the tables out and start playing music it has a nightclub vibe. Misty and Jo's uncle definitely capitalized off the whole Thirsty Thursday thing, too, inviting good DJs to play their sets here and making the drinks half price.

"What happened with Rebecca? The reality didn't meet your expectations?"

"You can say that."

"Or have you finally decided to open your eyes and realize you're in love with Barnes?"

My gaze swings to his blue eyes. "What?"

"Don't worry, your secret is safe with me, not that it's much of a secret, considering everyone fucking knows."

"What are you talking about? Who's talking about this?"

"Everyone in the locker room."

"I haven't heard anyone say anything." I feel myself frown as I set my empty glass down.

"Because no one wants those hands." Colson raises an eyebrow. "But trust me, they're talking."

"Brian's the one who's been out with her multiple times."

"And he hasn't gotten very far."

"That doesn't mean anything."

"It wouldn't if he hadn't said every time they're out she's texting or talking to you on FaceTime."

"That was one fucking time."

The Rulebreaker

"Bri's a good boy from the South. You think he's going to exaggerate that or make it up?"

I press my lips together. Do I think that? No. Do I think he's an asshole for telling my teammates that Rocky and I spoke a couple of times during their dates? Absolutely. I look at Colson again.

"Maybe if he actually paid attention to her like he should she wouldn't have been talking to me in the first place."

"Maybe." Colson shrugs a shoulder. "Or maybe he knows there's no competition between you and him and you already have her, so what's the point in trying?"

"Spoken like a true loser."

"It seems like everyone is a loser in this scenario. Brian for liking someone he can't have, you for liking someone you don't have the balls to go after, and her for pining after you with those puppy dog eyes and not giving anyone else a shot."

"What. The. Fuck. Are you talking about right now, Bridges?" I turn to him fully now, pulse racing. He must really be looking for a fight tonight.

"I'm just saying, Cruz. If you don't want her, tell her. Straight up. You're the most stand-up guy I know. Even on that TikTok we did, everyone said you're the one they'd want their daughter to date because they know that, but what you're doing is kind of fucked up."

"What am I doing? I'm not doing anything." I take a deep breath to calm down because this shit is exasperating.

"You're leading on your best friend and that's a sucky situation to be in if you're Rocky."

"You're talking like you've been in this situation."

"I have." He lets out a laugh. "Robin was my best friend and I fell hard for her and swallowed my feelings and where's Robin now?"

I cringe. "Married."

"Married," Colson confirms. "I mean, good for her, her husband's a great guy, but what the fuck? It just makes you wonder, what if I'd told her how I felt, you know?"

"Well, soon you'll be playing in the NHL and Robin will be wondering the same thing," I say, because I've seen the way she looks at Colson when her husband's not paying attention.

"An NHL contract doesn't mean shit if you don't have the right people to celebrate with." He raises an eyebrow. "A wise man once said that to me."

I take a breath and let it out, letting myself glance over at Rocky and Landon, who are talking. It's not that I wouldn't kill to be with her, because I would, but I'm not going to be the reason she doesn't play the field. Rocky got here with a few things in mind. She was going to play soccer, get a professional contract to play for a U.S. team, and enjoy the college experience, which, to her, includes hooking up with random guys. As far as I know, the only guy has been me and I'm not random. I took her virginity the other day, for God's sake, and I will never, for as long as I live, forget that night, but I refuse to bind her to me because of it. So, while I did say that, I've said it several times to my teammates and brothers—Jagger, who went pro, and Mitchell who will most likely go pro—and I truly believe it myself, but I want Rocky to be the one to decide I'm her forever and not the other way around. I don't want her to spend the rest of her life regretting that she ended up marrying the same guy she lost her virginity to and feel like she's trapped because of it.

Real love sucks sometimes.

Chapter Twenty-Four

Rocky

It's past two in the morning when I awaken at the feel of my bed shifting. I let out a long breath. Maverick has always been a terrible sleeper. When we were teenagers, he would call me in the middle of the night sometimes and we'd talk for hours until he found sleep. This is similar, except he doesn't always talk when he comes in here. Most of the time, he just lays beside me and falls asleep at some point. Some of the times, I don't even notice he's there until I wake up in the morning. We're both militant sleepers and don't move much, so despite his size, it's not like our paths cross while we're in bed. At least, they didn't, until the other night. I shut my eyes tighter and push the thought away. The last thing I need is to think about having sex with him right now. Just because he's hot and lying down beside me doesn't mean I have to touch him. I think I make a sound, a soft whimper, because suddenly he shifts again.

"Rock?"

"Hm?"

"You're awake?"

"No."

He chuckles. "Why are you lying?"

"Because I want you and it's ridiculous since I already decided I am not hooking up with you again."

"Hm." He reaches for me, his large hand landing on my hip. I swear my entire body goes haywire, the mere touch eliciting electricity to shoot through me. "You wanna tell me how you reached that conclusion?"

I turn to face him fully, his hand gliding over my abs, to the other hip. "You want me to date other guys."

"I do."

"Which means you don't want me to date you."

"It's a little more complicated than that."

"Explain."

"I want you to have the freedom to do what you want. You remember what you described your college experience like?"

"No." I let out a laugh.

"You said you wanted to do all the things you couldn't do when you were living with your parents. You wanted to go wild, within reason, and date a ton of guys since you hadn't thus far."

"Maybe I changed my mind."

He lets out a huffed laugh. "As much as I wish you did, and as much as I wish you'd say you're serious about me and dating me, I think you need to experience it for yourself."

"If you want to date other girls, you can just say that, you know?"

"That's not the case though. That's not what I'm saying."

I inch closer, until we're nearly chest to chest and I can feel the rest of his warmth against me. God, to have him this close. It's intoxicating. And still, here he is, practicing restraint. Restraint he normally doesn't practice with others. I understand it now though, so I'm doing my best not to get upset. I push closer still, my pelvis against his growing erection.

"Mav," I whisper.

"I'm trying so hard to be good, Rocky." His grip tightens on my hip. "Why are you doing this?"

"Because I can't stop. And you came into my room."

"I always come into your room."

"I know, but it's different now."

"So it did change things between us," he says.

"In a good way though."

"A good way?" He huffs out a breath that hits me on the forehead. "I don't know what's good about any of this."

I reach down and cup him over his thin gray pants.

"Jesus, Rocky." He groans loudly.

"Are you going to stop me?" I whisper against his throat.

"No, but I should. You should."

"I don't want to." I lower his cotton sleeping pants and find that he's not wearing underwear.

I've always wondered about that but never asked because it felt intrusive. Now I know. I palm his balls before moving onto his cock. I push him so that he's flat on his back and lower myself to take him in my mouth. This is something I've done before. Not a ton of times, but enough that I know what I'm doing, and from the sounds Mav is making when I add my mouth to my hand movement, I know I'm on the right track. His fingers disappear into my hair and he tugs hard, making me moan against him. He picks up his body and starts to fuck my mouth, keeping me steady with his hands on the top of my head. I feel my eyes fill with tears after a moment because he's so big and I'm not sure I can take any more, but pleasing him is making me wet, and I keep going. Suddenly, he pulls me off him and looks down at me with bewildered eyes.

"Come here."

I wipe my mouth and crawl up toward him, undressing as I move, until only my panties are left. Maverick puts his hands on my ass and hoists me up to his face so that I'm practically sitting on him. My body is burning, yearning for him to do something, but all he does is hold me there, breathing, exhaling onto me, tickling me through the thin layer of my panties. I'm so wet I can hardly take it, and when he hooks a finger through my panties and pulls them aside, letting his tongue hit my clit, I start to shake uncontrollably. It should be embarrassing, the fact that he hasn't done anything to elicit this orgasm from me, but it's not, and he keeps going, licking me like I'm his favorite ice cream, sucking me into his mouth like he can't let anything go to waste.

My body has a mind of its own as I start grinding against his face. This is something I've never done before, and it strikes me that this is the kind of thing he thinks I may want to experience with someone else. I just don't understand why? Why would I want that when he's so fucking good at what he's doing? I feel the orgasm build, crawling up through my toes and through my body as I arch my back and squirm, screaming his name. I try to be quiet, but it's no use, there's no hope for that. As I come down from it, Maverick brings me down his body slowly and turns me so that now I'm on my back and he's on top of me. His hands brush stray hairs out of my face and he thrusts into me, inch by inch, slowly, looking into my eyes with each motion. I bite my lip hard because fuck, he's big, and hard, and it doesn't hurt at all this time. He just feels so damn good. He brings a hand between us and starts to play with my clit and suddenly it's all too much and I'm coming again, and again.

"Fuck, baby, I'm close," he murmurs against me. "I'm going to . . ."

He pulls out of me before I can say anything and sputters all over my stomach. When we both catch our breaths, he pulls back.

"Don't move." He climbs off me, jogs to the bathroom, and comes back with a wet towel, which he uses to wipe me.

It's all a blur from there, me getting up to use the bathroom, him beside me in there. When we get back in bed, both dressed, he throws an arm over me and kisses the top of my head.

"I love you, Rocky."

"Love you too, Mav," I say, tears in my eyes as I close them.

It isn't unusual for us, to say we love each other, because we do, and that's how I know he's not going to let this go to the next level. He's too afraid of losing me to make me his girlfriend and I'm too afraid to lose him to push.

Chapter Twenty-Five

"Y ou should've had that one dammit," Leyla screams.

"I know!" I'm running back, dribbling the soccer ball down the field.

"There are scouts here. You need to get your shit together. Now," she yells back, running up to me and taking the ball from my feet to give it to Ashley, who will start the play over.

I put my hands on my hips and take a breath while they do. I'm a thousand percent distracted and I can't afford to be. Before the game, Mav texted me that he's taking Rebecca to the Halloween party. I texted that I was okay with it, but I wasn't, I'm not, and now it's the only thing I can think about when I'm supposed to be out here playing my heart out and securing my fucking future. There are already seventy minutes on the clock and most of us are running a little slower, taking short breaks between one goal and the other. The day is full of gloom, and the overcast sky is not doing us any favors either. I pick up the pace and run alongside Leyla. Morgan has the ball now and is setting the pace, which I'm grateful for. Morgan takes her time. She's all about the long game and getting us in the best position to score, rather than just running up the field and going for it.

I turn and run the route I've run thousands of times at practice, but the opponent won't leave me open for long. I side-step, waiting near the goal, then run to the open spot in front of it when Ashley takes control of the ball and kicks it in my direction—a long, high drive that sends it up, but not far enough to score it. I jump up, my opponent jumps with me, crashing into my shoulder, but my attention is just on the ball. I head butt it as hard as I can, and come down crashing, my opponent beneath me. I hear the yells and cheers and I know somehow, in the midst of the chaos, I scored the goal. I lay there catching my breath. My opponent starts to get up.

"You good?"

"Yeah." I nod just as Leyla runs over to help me up with Ashley, Morgan, and a few others running behind them screaming.

"You did that," Leyla screams. "You fucking did that."

"Did it look good? I couldn't even see." I laugh.

"It was ESPN worthy," Morgan says laughing.

We only have a second to enjoy it because we have to get right back to it. The game ends one to zero. Afterward,

Coach has words for us, and when she's done, I soak in one of the ice-filled tubs alongside Leyla and Morgan, who are talking about tonight's Halloween bash.

"I'm going as a pirate," I say. "I got this costume last year after Halloween, and I've been looking forward to wearing it since."

"I'm going as Peter Pan," Leyla says and continues talking when Morgan and I laugh loudly. "I'm not kidding. It's cute!"

"I'm going as a sexy flight attendant, you know, since we couldn't fly last year," Morgan says.

"I'm not sure what that has to do with your costume," I say, "but I'm sure you'll look great."

"What's Ashley going as?" Morgan asks.

"No idea," I say.

"Ummm . . . I wanna say she's going as Dorothy from the Wizard of Oz." Leyla shrugs. "I don't know."

"Are Maverick and Colson going?" Morgan asks.

"I think so." I close my eyes. "I'm dying to get out of here already."

"Same." Leyla laughs.

"So, you and Maverick," Morgan says. "Are the rumors true?"

"What rumors?" My eyes pop open. I glance over at Morgan.

"I heard you were sort of seeing each other." She smiles. "Which, I mean, freaking finally, right?"

"Excuse me, you didn't tell me this," Leyla says. "Since when?"

"Since never." I take a breath and exhale loudly. "We hooked up but it doesn't mean anything. I mean, it does, but it doesn't, you know?"

"No, I don't know." Leyla places both arms on the side of her tub and looks at me expectantly.

"What does that mean?" Morgan faces me as well.

"It means I'm probably going to be in love with my best friend until I find someone else to fall in love with."

The two of them exchange looks, then look at me again.

"I mean . . ." Morgan starts, looking unsure.

"You need to start by moving out and staying away from him for a while."

"Yeah, I'll start next week. I'm supposed to go to Charlotte next weekend with his family for Jagger's football game." I wipe my face and with a groan, I realize that I'm actually crying.

"Shit," Morgan says. "I'm sorry, Keke."

"It's fine. I mean, it's not like there's a solution, right?"

Not a winning solution, anyway, but ignoring him seems like the only viable option right now and that's what I'm going to try to do. It just absolutely sucks to ignore your best friend.

Chapter Twenty-Six

I LOOK DOWN AT MY PHONE AND SEE A FOURTH TEXT FROM Maverick.

Mav: What the hell is up? You haven't responded to my texts. I'm about to call you.

Me: Been busy.

Mav: You coming to the party?

Me: Yeah, I'll be there.

I stuff the phone in my black fanny pack and zip it back up. I'm not lying about being busy after my game and I am buzzing with the news but I want to tell Maverick in person, not via text or phone call or FaceTime. In person. I walk out of the bathroom and into Leyla and Ashley's living room, where they're both waiting for me, looking at their phones.

"Um, hello, how does this look?" I ask after a moment.

The Rulebreaker

"Hot," Leyla says.

"So hot, but I would definitely break the stockings a little more," Ashley says, walking over to me and crouching down to rip holes into my already holey stockings. "There."

"Thanks." I smile as I look down.

The skirt is extremely short, but that's the point of Halloween, right? Ashley and Leyla grab their purses and follow me outside, locking the door behind us. We decide to take an Uber, rather than drive, just in case any of us decides to drink tonight. We can usually bet on Ashley drinking, but Leyla and I are in celebration mode right now, so who knows what will happen.

When we get to the sorority house, I'm the first to say I'm glad we didn't drive here. It is the most crowded of any party this year and everyone seems to be in costume. The three of us get down and start walking toward the house.

"Val said to meet her on the side of the house by the kegs," Leyla says.

Val is one of the sorority girls and Leyla's current potential girlfriend. She calls her wifey during FaceTimes and Val seems like she loves it, so I don't think this is one of Leyla's "I thought I liked her, but just kidding" girls. Ashley and I look around as Leyla leads the way. Some of the costumes are definitely cool, much cooler than our store-bought costumes, but we barely have time to think, let alone make something out of scratch (which, let's be honest, we don't know how to do anyway).

"Oh, look, there's Brian, I think," Ashley says, pointing in the direction of a guy dressed like a Ghostbuster. "Oh, and Colson and Maverick!"

The fourth Ghostbuster is another guy from their hockey team and all of them look hot as fuck. The unbuttoned jumpsuit is something I totally would have made fun of Mav for if it weren't for that. His perfect abs on display aren't something to sneeze at though.

"Who would've thought those costumes could be hot?" Ash asks. "We should've done that."

"I think we're pretty naked and we look amazing."

"Rocky," Maverick calls out, followed by the other three shouting, "Rocky, Rocky, Rocky, Rocky."

"Oh my God." I cover my face with a groan, but can't help my laugh. "They're so embarrassing."

"Rockyyyyyy," Maverick shouts.

"Hold on!" I shoot him a look, but keep smiling as I jog over there.

Thank God I opted to wear low heel boots and not the stripper heels that Leyla was trying to sell me on, which looked great, but I would have definitely face-planted wearing them.

"Where have you been all day?" Maverick throws his arms around me and pulls me close.

"I had a game, remember?" I pull away and tilt my head to look at him.

"You look beautiful."

My stomach flutters.

"Awww," the guys around us say. I feel my skin grow hot.

"You do," Mav says. "You look fucking beautiful, my little pirate."

"My?" Colson says. "When did this happen?"

Maverick shoots him a look.

"What? I'm just asking for a friend." Colson shrugs a shoulder.

"Several friends, actually," Brian chimes in.

"Dad, you're embarrassing me." I slap a hand over my forehead and shimmy out of Maverick's hold.

"I have never been into that kink, but you can call me daddy whenever you want." His gaze heats as he takes me in. "And wearing that? Fuck yes."

"Oh my God." My jaw drops. "Maverick."

"What?"

"Are you drunk?"

"He's drunk," Colson says. "Sorry. He's a lightweight and he just took five shots back-to-back."

"Jesus," I breathe. "I mean, I guess it's good that he can blame this display on that?"

"No, babe, he always feels this way, he's just finally letting his feelings out," Colson says with a wink.

"I hate you."

"Keke," Maverick says. "Do you love me? Are you riding?"

"Oh my God." I start to laugh, then grab his hand and pull him away from the group. "I'll bring him right back, guys."

"She's going to do dirty things to me," Maverick calls out over his shoulder. "I hope."

"What has gotten into you?" I ask, letting go of his hand when we're far enough away from everyone.

"Nothing." He frowns. "Why?"

"You're being weird. Saying all these weird things in public."

"You want to keep me your dirty little secret? Because I will be." He reaches for me.

"No." I yank my hand away. "Can you focus for one second or not?"

"Yes." He takes a deep breath and lets it out. "Okay, I'm ready. Are you going to tell me why you've been avoiding me all day?"

"That's what I'm trying to do."

"Okay. I'm ready. For real this time." He grins.

"I have a boyfriend."

His smile drops, mood morphing from silly to crestfallen in a split second. "What?"

"I'm just kidding." I punch him on the chest playfully. "But now I know that you don't approve of that news."

"That's not funny, Rocky." He frowns. "At all."

"I was just kidding, dude. Chill." I roll my eyes. "Can I tell you the real news now?"

"Yeah, I guess, but you just absolutely killed the buzz I had going."

"Aw, sorry." I smile wide, but deep down, I am shaking because Maverick does care if I get a boyfriend. That's good to know.

"What's the news?"

"The NWSL invited me to try out for them," I say and can't help my squeal at the end of it.

"What?" he shouts, bringing his hands to his head. "What? I knew it, baby. I fucking knew it!"

"It's just a try-out." I jump up and down, smiling, laughing, and add, "But still!"

"They're going to sign you day one." Maverick is still shouting as he wraps his arms around me and lifts me off my feet, spinning me around. When he stops spinning, he buries his face on the side of my neck and murmurs, "This is your dream, baby."

"I know."

"I'm so fucking proud of you." He pulls away, still carrying me, and looks into my eyes. "I really am, Rocky. This is your time to shine. You earned this. Congratulations."

"Thank you." I'm still smiling, but I feel my eyes welling up. "I wanted you to be the first person I told but I didn't want to do it over the phone or text."

"You haven't told your parents?"

I shake my head. "Only you. Well, Leyla knows since they also extended an invitation to her."

"I'm the first one you told?"

"Yes, dummy. Best friends for life and all that." I smile.

"Yeah, best friends for life," he says, his voice lower, his gaze a little more distant as he sets me back on my feet. He smiles again. "I'm so happy for you."

"Thanks." I smile.

"Let's go take a shot to that!" he says excitedly again, and holds my hand as we walk back to our friends.

Chapter Twenty-Seven

THE INVITATION MEANS MORE PRACTICE AND MORE TRAINING. I've spent the entire week working on every single move and improving my techniques, to the point that I didn't even show up for my classes so far this week, something my parents do not approve of. Still, the time away from Maverick and everyone else has given me some clarity on our situation and that is—if it happens, it happens. If it doesn't, I'm okay with it. I'm not sure how that'll be once it's actually tested and put into action, but so far, in my mind, I'm good with just staying friends with him and nothing else. Leyla doesn't believe me. Neither does my own mother.

It doesn't matter though because after all the flirting and declarations he made at the party Saturday night, he practically ghosted me. He never came home that night, or Sunday, and by Monday I decided it was best because if I saw him, I would probably end our friendship and then it would've really been for nothing since we're no longer hooking up. For real this time.

I'm preparing a smoothie when I hear Maverick and Colson walk in talking about their game Friday night, and when I see him, I know my body didn't get the memo about the moving on and no longer hooking up thing, because he's not wearing a shirt and I can't handle it. I tear my eyes away from his naked chest quickly and finish blending my smoothie.

"You've been lost," Maverick says, his gaze swinging from me to the fridge as he opens it. I hate that we ever hooked up at all because of exactly this.

"Yeah, so have you. What's up with Friday?" I ask.

"Game is canceled. Some idiot on the other team got sick and got everyone else sick, so now they can't travel."

"Damn, that sucks." I look at the back of Maverick's head, or rather, his muscular back. "At least your parents won't have to be so tired for Charlotte the next morning."

"Right. Well, they want to go Friday afternoon now because of this. Can you still go or are you busy?"

"Is this your way of hoping I cancel?"

"Why would I want you to cancel, Rocky?" He shuts the door of the fridge and looks at me again. There's no light in his eyes, no excitement, if anything he looks bothered that I'm still standing here. I put away the blender, wash the blade, and pick up the cup I'm drinking from.

"I'll call your mother and let her know I can't come," I

say on my way out of the kitchen. I head to my room, shut the door, and lock it for good measure.

Fuck him.

After drinking my smoothie, I shower, put my pajamas on, and go straight to sleep. I hear music playing in the house but I'm too tired to care where it's coming from or what the reason is. If Mav is hooking up with some girl, that's fine by me. It hurts, but it's fine. I can't sit around waiting for a zebra to change its stripes. In the morning, I text Milly to let her know I can no longer make it on the trip.

Milly: You okay? We don't mind waiting and going Saturday as planned

Me: I'm good. I don't know if Mavy told you, but I'm trying out for the NWSL and I've been training all week

My phone starts buzzing in my hand and I smile when I see Milly's face on the screen. It's an old picture of the three of us—Milly, Mav, and me when we were getting ready to go to my prom. I've always loved those pictures, but now they kind of break my heart. I take a breath before answering.

"Hey."

"Congratulations, Miss Thing. I am so proud of you, baby!"

"Thank you." I smile wide.

"Your mother told me she had exciting news, but I thought she was talking about herself."

"I mean, she might have more exciting news." I laugh lightly. "It's just a try-out."

"They are going to sign you the first day!"

I laugh. "That's what Mav said."

"That kid talks my ear off and he didn't even mention this to me. I can't believe him."

"Well, he has a lot going on. I'm sure it slipped his mind."

"Now we have to wait until Saturday to leave. We have to celebrate this in Charlotte!"

"I would hate for you to wait for me." I bite my lip. "I should be done Friday at noon."

"So, we can still leave Friday. It's only a two-and-a-half-hour trip!"

"Okay."

"Do you not want to go?" she asks. "Because that's fine too, but if this is about Mav, don't you worry about him. Mitch is coming, Misty is coming, Jo will be there, obviously, I'll be there, Rob will be there. The last person you'll have to hang out with is Mav."

"It would be kind of weird if I go on a trip with you guys and ignore him." I laugh lightly again because this is such an awkward conversation to be having with his mother.

"I assume you're fighting, but I don't want to pry. He's sounded off the entire week. Not that it's any consolation."

"It's not," I say. "I don't like knowing he's going through things and feels like he can't talk to me about them."

"This is what it's like. We push the people we love most away all the time because we think we're shielding them from the pain, but all we're doing is creating more of it."

I swallow. "It sucks."

"I know, love. So, Friday night is a yes, right? Rob is renting a party bus."

"I'll be there." I laugh. "I can't miss a party bus!"

"Right? That's what I'm saying."

"Thanks, Milly. Talking to you always helps."

"I'm always here. Mav is my son and I love him, but even if he wasn't in the picture, I'd be here for you. I hope you know that."

"I do."

"Okay. See you soon! Love you."

"Love you."

When we hang up, I start to cry. This extended family that I adore so much is another thing I'm going to lose if I lose my friendship with Mav. I know Milly means it when she says she'll always be there for me, but it'll be different.

It's always different.

Chapter Twenty-Eight

WE ALL PILE INTO THE PARTY BUS AFTER SAYING OUR HELLOS to one another. Milly grabs my hand and Misty's and announces we're sitting in the back and tells the guys to be in charge of the playlist for the first hour of the trip. We'll be in charge the second hour. It's just as well. I wouldn't know what to play and I'd end up playing whatever Maverick listens to since he's practically in charge of the playlist at the house anyway. As the three of us head to the back, I glance over at Misty, who looks at me at the same time and shoots me a "this will be interesting" look. I smile. We sit down—Misty, Milly, and me—in the back row of the bus.

"Well, if you've ever wanted to try out stripping," I say, looking at the pole in front of us.

"Been there, done that. It's actually a really good workout," Milly says.

I laugh. "Oh my God."

"I saw the funniest video about a guy saying that if we want to learn to strip we should go to the strip club and have an actual stripper teach us," Misty says. "I thought about it until I remembered that the only time I've ever been to a strip club was with these idiots and I wanted to die." She looks at us. "With the baseball team, I mean."

"You couldn't pay me enough to go to any kind of club with the baseball team," Milly says.

"Yeah. Lesson learned." Misty crosses her arms, then looks over at me. "So, professional soccer, huh?"

"It's just a try-out. I don't want to get my hopes up." I bite my lip.

"They're going to sign you," Milly says.

"Yeah, you can't think like that. Manifest that shit, girl," Misty adds. "You're going to get a badass contract and travel everywhere. How exciting." She smiles wide. "What does Mavy think about losing his best friend?"

I know Misty and I know it's a genuine question, but the words are all wrong right now and I feel a punch in the gut from it. My eyes well up without warning and I wipe them quickly, letting out a breath.

"I'm sorry. I didn't mean that in a bad way at all," Misty leans over and sets a hand on mine. "I think it's safe to say you guys have an unbreakable friendship."

"Is that what you're worried about?" Milly asks. "You guys losing your friendship when you join the real world? You know that won't happen."

"It's a lot of things." I wipe my face. "I guess I just don't like change as much as I thought I did. The unknown is scary."

"Terrifying." Misty squeezes my hand. "But the one thing I know you'll always be able to count on is having Mav in your life and us. I know we don't hang out much aside from random run-ins at parties, but I always got your back. I hope you know that."

"Thanks." I smile and take another deep breath. "I don't know why I'm crying."

"Oh, honey." Milly wraps an arm around me and hugs me to her side. "You've always been such a good girl."

"Maybe that's the problem," I say with a laugh.

"Hey, it may be. You need to do something rebellious this weekend," Milly says. "But not too rebellious. I don't want Ms. Bev and Mike knocking on my door."

I laugh loudly. "Oh, God. They would."

"You know they would." Milly laughs.

"One of my favorite memories is still when I went to New York that summer and your mom had us all over for curry chicken and rice and peas. So good. It became my favorite food, actually." Misty smiles.

"She'll be so happy to hear that," I say. "She always

talks about Milly's mangú. We've tried to make it, but it just doesn't turn out the same."

"According to Mavy you've got it on lock," Milly says.

"Yeah, well, Mavy would eat a truck and call it gourmet."

We all laugh. The rest of the trip is spent talking about other things—like Misty's senior project, which is an article on college athletes, and Milly trying to convince her to go work for their magazine when she graduates. Then, we talk about fashion and scroll social media for clothes. It's the most relaxing, fun time I've had in a long time.

When we get to Charlotte, we get off the highway and go up winding roads lined with beautiful magnolia trees. Every so often, I spot a huge gate that I'm sure leads to a mansion. At the end of the road, we stop in front of one and Roberto lowers his window, types in a code, and the gates open. It's another long road before we reach the mansion. Once we're parked, we all get out of the bus. Mitchell and Maverick are bickering back and forth about basketball. Neither of them plays basketball, but I swear they're obsessed with the NBA nonetheless. Roberto is checking a tire. Misty is on her phone. Milly is going through her purse. I'm just trying hard not to freak the hell out because this is the biggest house I've ever seen in my life. The Cruzes are very well off, they have multiple properties in New York, one in LA, one in Miami, a couple in the Dominican Republic. But none of their properties are like this. This is a legitimate estate. The kind of stuff none of the brown people I know would ever have the opportunity to own. Yet, Jagger and Josephine own it. The thought fills me with pride.

"This is insane," I say when I can pick my jaw up off the floor.

"Ridiculous," Misty adds. "Wait till you see my sister's closet. It's a dream."

"It's ridiculous," Milly says with a smile. "But, hey, good for them."

"I mean, it's beautiful, but all I can think about is the upkeep."

"I wouldn't be able to do it," Milly says. "And I live in a penthouse in New York, which is not cheap, but this is another level of responsibility. Jo hasn't even been able to do anything for herself yet because she's been so caught up in housework."

"She likes it though," Misty responds with a shrug. "My sister's weird. She's all about her career, but deep down she wants to be a housewife."

"You think so?" Milly laughs.

"I mean, she'd never admit it." Misty smiles as we walk up to the giant doors.

The right side opens fully and Jo and Jagger appear, all smiles, to greet us.

"You made it," Jo says, and we all exchange hugs and kisses. "Excuse me, Keke, I heard you're going pro. I'm going to need you to sign something for me before you get all big."

"It's a try-out," I say, then correct myself when I find Misty and Milly shooting me a look, "but yes, I'm going pro and I'm going to play for the United States Women's National Soccer League and become famous, so I'll sign something for you now."

"Daaamn," Jagger and Mitchell both say, "this calls for a celebration!"

"Come here, little sis." Jagger throws his arms around me. "I'm proud of you. Do you have an agent? I can hook you up—"

"Jag. I haven't even given her a tour of the house and you're already all business?" Jo says, raising her eyebrow. "Chill, dude."

"Sorry, dude." Jagger kisses his fiancée on the lips, a loud, long peck that makes me smile.

It's wild to see them together like this considering I never in a million years saw it coming. I guess now when I look back at the times we all hung out together, I can say I saw some signs of attraction there, but this is next level. They have a house together, they're getting married soon, and they are obviously super in love. They're really living the dream. I love it. I've tried my best not to look in Maverick's direction for the last three hours, but as we continue walking into the house, I glance over and catch him looking at me. Butterflies swarm my core immediately. I wish I could push them down and make them go away, but I know it's unlikely. I spent the entirety of the week trying to stay away from him, but I'm starting to think that no amount of time can pacify these feelings.

Chapter Twenty-Nine

Maverick

We're in Jagger's massive game room, playing darts—myself, Jagger, Mitchell, and Dad—while the girls are marveling over Jo's closet, if I had to guess. There's a laundry room downstairs that's easily the size of at least three one-bedroom New York apartments dedicated to all of Josephine's clothes. She can't even fill it, that's how big it is, but I guess with my brother's new contract, she'll have no trouble filling it soon, if she wanted to.

"What's up with you?" Dad asks, standing beside me as he prepares to shoot darts next.

"With what?"

"How do you feel about Rocky potentially, most likely, getting a professional contract?"

"I feel great about it, obviously." I frown as I look over at him. "Why?"

"I don't know. It'll change things. She'll be gone a lot." Dad throws a dart and hits the outside corner of the board. I'm kind of glad he's not great at something for once.

"I'll be going pro soon, too. I'm signing as a free agent the minute the season is over. Maybe before then."

"You decided?" Dad turns to me. He's a huge man, but not bigger than me, not anymore anyway. When I was little I used to think of him as a bear, muscular and warm. I still think of him like that, but now I'm also a full-grown bear, and being beside him like this always reminds me of that.

"I did. If I do the accelerated program that I was accepted into, I can be done with classes by the summer, so I'll get the degree you guys want me to get that I'll probably never use, and I'll hopefully get a decent contract."

"Decent?" Dad chuckles, then turns to my brothers, who are examining Jagger's liquor collection, which he probably hasn't even touched yet. "Guys, your brother thinks he may have a chance at a decent contract in the NHL."

"Decent?" Jagger laughs.

"Bro, shut the hell up. You'll be able to buy this mansion twice," Mitch says with a laugh, then looks at Jag. "Not that there's anything wrong with this mansion."

"You think I'm going to take offense to that?" Jagger shakes his head with a smile. "Imagine Grandpa's face if he were alive to see this. I think about that a lot, you know? Our grandparents didn't have money to afford shoes, and look at us. It's borderline exorbitant."

"It's not borderline exorbitant, Jag. It is exorbitant," Dad says.

"Damn, we're blessed," Mitch adds with the shake of his head.

"We are, and don't you ever forget it," Dad says. "So, what does Drew say about the free agency thing? Do I need to speak to him?"

"No, Dad. I'm an adult." I shoot the dart and hit the middle target. Drew is Jagger's agent, and will be mine the minute I can sign.

"Right, but do I need to speak to him?" Dad raises his eyebrow.

"I guess you can." I roll my eyes.

My dad's never going to let me sign anything without looking at it first, so there's no point in pretending that would ever be the case. It's a good thing, though. I'm fortunate to have people who know sports contracts beside me.

"Do you know where you'll sign? You had a few teams interested," Mitch says.

"Not yet."

"Tell me you're waiting for the girl you're in love with to sign to a city first, without telling me you're waiting for the girl you're in love with to sign. I'll go first," Jagger says, smirking.

"Fuck you. I'm not waiting for that." I shoot him a glare.

"But you are in love with her." Mitch looks way too pleased that he caught me in that one.

"I'm not going to deny it." I shrug a shoulder.

"What?" Dad nearly shouts, then laughs. "When did this happen? Is that why she's avoiding you like the plague?"

"Something like that."

"Damn, dude. Don't fuck this up. Keke is like your soul mate," Jag says.

"He's not wrong," Mitch adds, still looking at the alcohol in front of him. "This looks expensive."

"Did you tell her you're in love with her?" Dad asks.

"No. I just . . . I don't know. We sort of hooked up and then I told her she should date other people."

"What?" Dad looks bewildered. "Who the fuck does that?"

"And why?" Mitchell adds, looking equally as bewildered.

"You are so weird," Jagger says.

"You're one to talk, Mister Let's-hook-up-casually-and-not-fall-in-love." I shoot him a look.

"Well, it worked out for me. I'm engaged."

"And you, Mister I'm-going-to-date-this-girl-and-fall-in-love-with-her-and-then-break-up-with-her-and-pine-after-her-forever." I shoot Mitchell a look.

"I was seventeen," Mitchell says as if that's any excuse for what he did. "I didn't know any better."

"I don't know how or where our parenting went wrong, but the three of y'all are a mess," Dad says, shaking his head.

"And here I thought your mother and I having a normal, stable relationship was enough."

"You kind of set the bar pretty high," I say.

My brothers mutter their agreement behind me.

"Well, I'm sorry for marrying my best friend and love of my life and having a good relationship with her."

"I don't know how you married your best friend," I say quietly. "It seems impossible."

"Yet here we are, thirty years later, still happy," Dad says. "Not to say we haven't had our share of trials and tribulations, but still, we truly are happy together."

My brothers and I exchange awkward glances. Once upon a time, our parents were headed toward divorce. They weren't quiet about it either, but they always did hold each other with the utmost respect and never spoke badly about one another. Still, it was hard to go through. That was around the time Mitchell broke up with Misty too, which always made me think the two were related in some way. I don't have time to dwell on that now though. I need to tell Rocky how I really feel and what I really want and leave the ball in her court.

"What have you done, Maverick Enrique Cruz?" Mom says when I bump into her on my way to my room.

"What are you talking about?" My heart stills in my chest.

I may be a man, but no amount of years will ever make me not be afraid of my mother when she says my full name in that tone.

"What did you do to Rocky?"

"What'd she say?" My eyes widen.

Oh fuck. If there's any chance I hurt Rocky and my mother finds out, I'm toast. She's always been very clear on her stance on girlfriends. She loves us and we're her kids but if we don't treat women with the utmost respect, we're in trouble. From the way she's looking at me, I know Rocky said something she didn't like, and Rocky isn't just a girlfriend. She isn't even my girlfriend, but I know better than to bring that fact up right now.

"What should she have said?" Mom raises an eyebrow and places a hand on her hip. My heart pounds faster.

"Mami, I didn't do anything, I swear."

"You think that because I let you off the hook most of the time it's okay to hurt a girl?"

"Hurt her?" My eyes widen even more, if possible. "I didn't hurt her. She hurt me."

"Really?" She laughs. "Please explain."

"I can't." I let my shoulders sag and look at the floor. "I don't want to talk about this with you right now."

"Because you don't want to tell me the truth about what happened."

"I guess." I look up at her. "But I didn't hurt her. Not on

purpose. You know I would never do that to anyone, especially not her."

"I know, but the fact remains that she's hurt. She tried to cancel this trip, you know."

"Yeah."

"Why's that?"

"Because I was being a jerk," I mumble, hating to admit that aloud.

"Why?"

"Because I'm in love with her but I don't want to tell her." I look away.

"Why the hell not, Maverick?"

"Because she needs to live a little. She needs to meet other guys." Even as I say the words I feel like throwing up. I hate—loathe—the idea of Rocky with another guy.

"So, she wants to be with you and you pushed her away because you think she needs to be with other guys?" Mom frowns deeply. "I must be missing something."

"I can't be her first serious boyfriend. You know those other clowns she dated weren't serious."

"Right." Mom laughs. "And why can't you be her first real boyfriend?"

"Because I want to marry her, Mom." The words surprise me, but not her, apparently. She just watches me, waiting for me to continue. "You're not supposed to marry your first real boyfriend. This isn't the 1940s."

"And because it isn't the 1940s, you shouldn't think that you need to make that decision for her."

I purse my lips. She's not wrong. I don't want to admit that, but really, she's not wrong. But Rocky doesn't know what she wants. She told me she wanted to date a bunch of guys. She told me she wanted to be free of her strict parents' rules.

"You need to tell her how you feel and let her make that choice for herself," Mom says, walking toward me and setting a hand on my shoulder and the other under my chin so I look at her, because even though I'm at least a foot taller than her, I'm not looking into her eyes. When I do, I feel instant comfort.

"What if I lose her? If I fuck this up, I'd lose her friendship. I don't know if I can live with that."

"So don't fuck it up." She smiles. "It's easier said than done, I know, but if you're true to yourself and respect her and love her the way you do, it'll be easier than you think."

I swallow, then wrap my arms around my mom and thank her. This is why I rely on her advice over my brothers. She always knows exactly what to say to make my thoughts less cloudy.

Chapter Thirty

Rocky

The bedroom I was assigned is right beside Maverick's, which makes me wonder how involved he was in the arrangement. It doesn't matter though, the rooms are huge and each have their own bathrooms. I mean, the house is insane. Not long after seven o'clock, there's a knock on my door, and I call out for whoever it is to come inside. When I see it's Maverick, my heart nearly explodes. He's already dressed for dinner, dark jeans, white sneakers, and a white short sleeved button-down. Mitch and Jo are having a chef over to cook for all of us, so I opted for casual as well and went with a white wrap dress with ruffled sleeves, that's a little short, but not too short, and white thong sandals. Misty and Jo are also wearing similar wrap dresses and Jo's is definitely sexier than mine so I feel comfortable with my choice.

"Wow," Mav says as he shuts the door behind him and walks forward. He brings a hand from behind him and walks toward me with a red rose in his hand. "I stole this from one of Jo's arrangements. Don't tell on me."

"I don't think she'll miss it." I smile, pulse racing as he reaches me and hands me the rose. "It's beautiful."

"You're beautiful." He searches my eyes as he says the words.

"Mav." I quiver and take a breath. "You can't keep saying things like that to me. I gave you a list to woo other women, not me."

"You're the only one I want to woo, though, Keke."

"You told me to date other guys."

"I know what I said, but I don't know if I can do this. I don't know if I can watch you with other guys anymore and act like I'm okay with it."

"Act like you're okay with it? So, you weren't okay with it before?"

"Of course not. I mean, I was fine with it because I love seeing you happy, but that doesn't mean I wasn't also wildly jealous."

"But you were my first."

"I know." He shuts his eyes in an exhale, as if savoring that. When he opens again, they're lava. "Which is why I was trying to resist this. Part of me wants to be an asshole and tell you that you're mine and never let you go, but you deserve to be with other guys. You deserve to be wooed and taken out."

"What if I don't want other guys? What if I want you to be that guy?"

He brings a hand down to cup my face, my neck. "What if you regret that later on?"

"Later on?" I let out a laugh. "You're talking like we're getting married."

"Like I said, what if you regret that later on?"

"Maverick." My chest flutters. "How will I know you're not going to change your mind again?"

"Because I'm telling you I won't." He reaches into the collar of his shirt and pulls out the necklace he's wearing.

"How did you . . . you still have it?" My eyes widen when I see the broken half heart that says BEST.

"I'm sure I do, but this is a new one." He reaches into his pocket and gives me the other half. I smile at the word FRIENDS. "You know I would never do anything to destroy what we have, right?"

"Our friendship, yeah, I have no doubt about that." I clasp the necklace in my grip. "But what about everything else?"

"I can't imagine I'd ever do anything to hurt the love of my life." He looks into my eyes. "Especially since the love of my life happens to be my best friend."

My bottom lip starts to quiver. "Mav."

"If I had it my way, I'd make you my wife right now, this second, but I know that sounds crazy and—"

"I like crazy," I say, smiling as I wipe my tears. "But I don't mind savoring this. We have a lot going on right now."

"I know." He licks his lips. "That's another thing I want to talk to you about. I know you're going to do your try-out and I know you're going to get offers from a lot of places, so I want you to pick whatever team you feel is best for you and I'll—"

I wrap my arms around his neck, pull my legs up and wrap them around his waist, and kiss him. "Stop being so serious for once, Mav." I pull away and smile. "By the way, I'm in love with you too. I've been in love with you for a while now, even if you're too blind to see it."

"Dammit, Rocky." He kisses me again, so deeply that I feel like I'm going to combust. When he pulls away, we're both breathing heavily. "I'm not letting you go. I hope you know that."

"I'm totally okay with it." I smile.

For the first time in a long time, I feel amazing.

Chapter Thirty-One

Maverick

"Misty," Jo says, walking into the kitchen from the other side. "I cannot believe you are such a freaking baby. You called Mom?!"

"You guys put me in a room that literally looks like UNC vomited in it, so yeah, I called Mom," Misty says, looking between Jo and Jagger. "What the hell?"

Jagger starts to laugh along with everyone else in there. I bite my tongue to keep from laughing because even though we're not in the kitchen just yet, hearing the commotion is hilarious. Misty attends a rival university, and that makes this even funnier.

"Unbelievable." Misty shakes her head, and as we walk into the kitchen, we see her turn her glare toward Mitch. "Keep laughing."

"Nope." Mitch straightens. He looks like he's dying to laugh, but is trying really hard to hold it in. "I'm good."

"Such a baby," Jo says again. "Mom and Dad think it's hilarious, by the way."

"Of course, they do. You're all traitors."

"You're the only one who chose Duke over UNC! You're the traitor," Jo shoots back.

"Oh, I see you kissed and made up," Mitchell taunts as Rocky and I walk into the kitchen hand in hand.

"You told them?" She squeezes my hand and looks up at me.

"Yeah, pretty sure no one here is surprised by this development," Mom says.

"I'm surprised," Dad says. "I mean, really, Rocky, you could do so much better."

Rocky laughs loudly and grips my hand again. "Honestly, Roberto, I gave it a lot of thought but after seeing what's out there, I somehow kept coming back to him."

"I joined a dating app recently, so I feel this on a deep level," Misty adds.

"You joined a what?" Mitchell shouts. "When? Why?"

"I got tired of going on dates with the same three guys." Misty shrugs a shoulder. "Jo put me on one, so blame her."

All eyes turn to Jo, who gasps. "You guys are so judgy. She needs a man in her life so she can stop calling me at one in the morning when she has all her high musings." Jo laughs. "Sorry, Misty. I guess everyone knows you smoke now."

"It's for anxiety," Misty says, eyes wide.

"Hey, you don't owe us an explanation," Mom says. "I smoke once in a while."

"What?" I roar alongside my brothers. "Mom, no!"

"My, how the tables have turned," Dad says with a laugh. "I told you they'd think you're a pothead."

"Not that there's anything wrong with being a pothead at my age." Mom shoots each of us a pointed look. "But it really does help me with my aches and pains once in a while, so, sorry, not sorry."

Rocky tries and fails to fight a laugh, especially when Jo and Misty start laughing uncontrollably, because admittedly, my brothers and I are in complete shock.

"This day is wild," I say after a moment. "Wild."

"Ma, we don't even drink!" Mitchell says, then corrects himself when all of us look at him, "I mean, not a lot anyway."

"We definitely don't do drugs," Jagger says. "I just can't believe that after all of those lectures you gave us . . . " He shakes his head.

"Relax." Mom rolls her eyes. "I dedicated my life to raising three healthy, yet annoying boys and started a couple of companies. If I want to relax once in a while with something that's not only legal, but natural, I'm allowed, dammit."

"It's not legal in this state," Jo adds. "Not that it stops Misty, as you can see."

"It's not my fault some states are behind on the times and would rather keep feeding big pharma and letting them control us and make us addicted to the opioids of their choosing," Misty argues.

"Holy shit. I need a drink because after this conversation I have a feeling we'll all need a little weed in our lives," Dad says, walking over to the small bar. He looks over at the chef, who has been laughing at our entire exchange the whole time. "I'm sure you've heard worse things."

"Much worse," the chef says.

"Let's talk about something less triggering," I say. "Like Jo and Jagger's wedding."

"Less triggering?" Jagger shouts with a laugh. "Dad, get me a drink, please, before Bridezilla starts going on her rants."

"I am not a Bridezilla, Jagger, what the fuck?" Jo says, crossing her arms over her chest.

"You sure you want to be part of this forever?" I ask Rocky, looking down at her. "I mean, you've already been part of this forever, but it'll be next level."

"I like next level." She reaches up and kisses my chin because that's as far as she can reach without heels. "I definitely like next level with you."

"Good." I let go of her hand and squeeze a handful of

her ass. "Because I still have a few things on that list to cross off."

"I mean, I can always make you a new list." She winks. "A naughtier one."

I close my eyes momentarily, trying to keep myself from reacting.

Yeah, taking this from friendship to relationship is definitely something I could never get over or regret.

Chapter Thirty-Two

Rocky

"I COME IN PEACE," Maverick shouts from the other side of the theatre.

I lower into my seat and try not to laugh. Last time he did this, I was the only person here. This time, we have company. They're sitting up near the front, but still, company. I shake my head as he walks down the row and reaches me.

"You're too loud for the theatre," I whisper as he sits down beside me.

"I thought about renting out a theatre for just the two of us." He leans in and kisses me. "But I know how important it is for you to watch the previews and I don't want to be a distraction."

I roll my eyes. "A little late for that."

The Rulebreaker

"Is it?" He raises an eyebrow. The lights dim. He leans in and whispers, "Why don't you come and sit on my lap?"

I raise an eyebrow. I'm wearing a plaid yellow and black skirt and crop top. It was another option for a Halloween costume, but I didn't use it and then I decided I didn't care if Halloween was over, I was still going to dress like Dionne. I set my popcorn down, stand up, walk between his legs, shutting my eyes and inhaling when his hands grip the back of my thighs and make their way up underneath my skirt.

"Fuck, Rocky, you're going to kill me with this," he whispers.

"Shh," I taunt quietly, but it doesn't matter, the previews are loud and the people up front are too far to hear us. I hope. I take a step back as he spreads my legs and guides me onto his lap, one hand on my waist, the other underneath my skirt, toying with the string hiding between my ass cheeks. He brings his lips to the side of my neck, licking, kissing, as he continues to move his fingers up and down the string, the front of my panties digging into my folds with each motion. I feel my breathing quicken.

"You like this, baby?" he whispers hotly in my ear. "You like when I play with your pussy like this? What if we get caught?"

For some reason, his words make me hungrier for him, and when his fingers begin stroking along my folds, outside of my panties and he groans against my ear, commenting on how wet I am, my body reacts. I start to move against his fingers with ease, gliding, and he lets me. He gives me full control of the pace. He bites down on my shoulder blade and I gasp, back arching, moving faster in search of release. I find it quickly, and just as I'm coming down from the orgasm, he tugs on my clit. A simple tug, torture, and I want more. I need more. He continues kissing my neck and makes his way up to the shell of my ear as his other hand leaves my waist and sneaks underneath my shirt and bra, cupping my breast, pinching my pert nipple.

"It's too much," I whisper. "I need you inside me."

"Hm." He moves a hand from underneath my skirt and adjusts himself underneath me.

I feel his cock on my lower back, straining against us, and I pick myself up from his lap just to give me enough room to grab it and guide it inside of me. It hurts. It always does. I'm so wet, but he's so big, and settling over him makes me feel so full. My arms shake on the armrest on either side of us as I pull myself up and back down.

"Fuck, baby. Just like that," he says into my ear. "Ride me just like that."

His hands go back to my waist, helping me do just that. My knees begin to buckle as he thrusts deep inside me, the wave of the impending orgasm washing through me all at once. I put a hand over my mouth so that I don't scream. I value this movie theatre too much to get kicked out forever. Yet, when his cock swells inside me and he rocks against me hard and fast, making my eyes roll to the back of my head, I can't find it in me to care about the consequences.

"The movie was good." Maverick shoots me a grin, reaching for my hand as we walk out of the theatre two hours later.

"You're unbelievable." I shake my head.

"I'm so glad you think so." He winks. I laugh. *This guy.* My phone vibrates and I answer my parents' call.

"So?" Mom asks. "Good, right?"

"It was good."

"It was great," Maverick adds beside me.

"Maverick saw it? Mavy, you hate the theatre," Mom says.

"Mom, he can't hear you." I shake my head even though she can't see me.

My mother thinks that because she walks around talking on speakerphone, everyone must do the same. It's an annoying habit I'm trying to get her to kick. After exchanging pleasantries with her and Dad, when we get in my car, I set the phone on speaker.

"Mavy, I thought you hated the movies?" Mom asks again, now that he's listening.

"I used to but it's definitely one of my favorite places now." Mav glances over, a smoldering look on his face. I shoot him a look and thank the Lord we're not on FaceTime with my parents.

"Did you like the movie?" Dad asks. "The show is really good."

"Dad's really into Anime now," I explain. "*Demon Slayer* is his favorite."

"There are others, but this is a good one to start with," Dad says.

"I don't think Maverick wants to get into it, Dad."

"You don't know that. Maybe I'll start watching." Mav shrugs a shoulder.

"Are you trying to kiss my ass since you're dating my daughter?"

Mav's eyes go wide. "No, sir."

"So, you're just trying to kiss my ass because you want to?"

"Um, I wasn't really trying to kiss your ass." Mav scratches the back of his neck. I laugh.

"Dad, leave him alone."

"What? Just because I've known him since before he hit puberty he's supposed to get special treatment?" Dad asks. "No, ma'am. He'll be treated like every other boyfriend. There is a trial period."

"What kind of trial period?" Mav asks.

"If I tell you then you'll prepare for it. Don't worry, you're doing all right so far," Dad says. "I don't agree with you luring her to move in with you so that you could seduce her though, let's be clear about that."

"Mike," Mom reprimands, laughing. "Stop it."

"What? It's true," Dad says. "In Jamaica we would never."

"Oh, here we go." I roll my eyes. "We're not in Jamaica, Dad. You're not even in Jamaica Queens, so don't even."

"And, Mike, if you remember correctly, that was exactly what you wanted to do with me, back in Jamaica," Mom says, her accent coming in strong.

"Uh-oh," Mav says, "I'm staying outta that one. When Momma Bev brings out the accent you know it's on."

"I think we can all agree that the movie was great," I say, jumping in before things get crazy.

"It was," Mav says.

"I thought it had too much violence," Mom says.

"Beverly," Dad starts.

"Nope. Don't tell me anything about that, Michael. I asked you about the violence and you said it was a cartoon. Well, cartoons can be violent, as we all saw."

I shoot Mav a look and sigh. He smiles and holds my hand.

"Are we done?" I ask.

"Yes," Mom says. "Love you, baby. Talk tomorrow."

"Love you, baby. Love you too, Maverick. Don't forget your manners around my daughter," Dad says.

"You know I won't, sir."

I hang up and slap a hand over my forehead. "They are the most."

"They love you." Mav smiles. "We all love you and want what's best for you, so you can't blame them for being the most."

"I love you, even though you did ask me to move in and then took advantage of me."

"Me?" Mav laughs. "As I recall, you were begging me to be your first."

"Ah, well, the details are murky."

"Unbelievable." He shakes his head, laughing. "So, where do you wanna go next?"

"I'm hungry."

"Me too."

"But I don't want Tony's. I think if I eat pasta again this month I'll never eat it again."

"No Tony's then." He laughs and starts driving.

I like having things figured out, but at the end of the day, I don't really care what I do so long as it's with him.

Chapter Thirty-Three

Maverick

Two Months Later

"Maverick, you're going to break my hand."

"Sorry." I loosen my grip on Rocky's hand. "I'm nervous."

"I don't know why." She smiles at me. "This is the team you want to play for."

"I know, I know, but this is the rest of my life."

"For now." She squeezes my hand. "It's a good contract and a good city. And you get to stay close to Jagger for a while."

"And it's the city you'll be playing for." I grin. "That's why it's a no-brainer."

"And because you like it." Rocky raises an eyebrow.

"Yeah, I do like it."

"Good. Now sign that contract and get paid, baby!"

So, I do, and it feels good to see my name on that paper. Carolina Hurricanes have no idea what they have coming, especially since Colson is also signing with them. Rocky signed with the North Carolina Courage and has been waiting for training to start with them soon. At first, I was surprised she picked them over New York or Florida, but we've made North Carolina our home these last few years here, so I'm glad she picked them and that we get to stay here longer. I would have picked Mars if that was where she said she was going, though. Anywhere with her.

Epilogue

Rocky

'M LYING ON THE GRASS, BREATHING IN THE FRESH AIR, WHEN I hear the door to the back of the house open and close. Mav set up a picnic for us in our new backyard and it's a dream, but he went back inside to get champagne for our orange juice to turn it into mimosas.

"The weather is perfect," I say.

"You're perfect."

I inhale and exhale, smiling. I don't think I've stopped smiling for almost a year now. "Did you talk to Jag? Did they finally settle on a summer wedding?"

"Yep. In the Dominican Republic. I don't know what possesses people to have destination weddings."

"At least it's a familiar destination." I shrug a shoulder.

"Hey, Rocky." I hear him pouring our glasses.

"Hm."

"Let's get married."

"What?" My eyes pop open. I look over to where he's sitting and sit up, turning to face him.

"My parents always say their friendship comes before everything, and Mom always said when looking for a partner, I should look for someone who can be my best friend," he says, shifting so that he's on one knee now and that's when I notice that he has a ring box in his hand. "I just never thought to look at you in that way because I was so afraid to lose you. When we were fourteen we went to that summer camp upstate and during that trip we promised we'd be in each other's weddings, remember?"

"Yes." I cover my mouth and let out a laugh, hoping against all hope that the tears will stop trickling down and ruining my makeup.

"Well, I still want to do that, but I want to move my position from best man to groom, if you'll have me. Rocky Barnes, I can't do life without you. You're my best friend, my soul mate, my everything. Please marry me."

"Jesus Christ, Maverick." I'm openly crying now as I nod. "Yes. Obviously. I mean, we just bought a freaking house together."

He laughs. "That's the only reason?"

"Shut up and put this crazy ring on my finger." I gasp as he does. "Oh my God. It's perfect."

"Just like you, bestie." He leans in, cups both sides of my

face, and kisses me. When he pulls away, he smiles. "I hope you don't mind that we have a bit of an audience."

When I look over to see what he's talking about, I see my parents, his parents, Jagger, Mitchell, Jo, Misty, Colson, and a few other friends standing there, and I start crying even harder. I laugh as I wipe my tears and look over at him. I've known him forever and I cannot wait to see where this journey will lead us.

ClaireContrerasbooks.com

Twitter:
@ClariCon

Insta:
ClaireContreras

Facebook:
www.facebook.com/groups/ClaireContrerasBooks

Other Books

The Trouble With Love

Fake Love

The Consequence of Falling

Because You're Mine

Half Truths

The Sinful King

Twisted Circles

Fables & Other Lies

The Heartbreaker

Second Chance Duet

Then There Was You

My Way Back to You

The Wilde One

The Player

THE HEART SERIES

Kaleidoscope Hearts

Torn Hearts

Paper Hearts

Elastic Hearts

DARKNESS SERIES

There is No Light in Darkness

Darkness Before Dawn

CPSIA information can be obtained
at www.ICGtesting.com
Printed in the USA
FSHW010030150721